Noah's Story

Bear Family, Volume 2

David Camily

Published by Ryan T. Osborn, 2022.

NOAH'S STORY

First edition. November 28, 2022.

Copyright © 2022 David Camily.

ISBN: 979-8215949306

Written by David Camily.

Also by David Camily

Bear Family
Mason's Story
Noah's Story
A Night at the Rainbow Rose

Bear Family Large Print Edition
Mason's Story

Watch for more at https://lordshiningstarr1.wixsite.com/davidcamily.

For Soleil

Chapter One

Noah Easton looked at the organized chaos with worry. The kitchen was swarming with people and starting to feel stuffy. Refreshments, check. Daddy Mason's mother, Carrie Dale, had a love affair with chocolate chip cookies. So Noah bought a tray of chocolate chip cookies and a meat tray. He grabbed the cookies from the fridge and placed them on the table. Next to them, the punch bowl was ready and waiting to be filled. Noah worried that Carrie would be upset that they'd used her good punch bowl for the punch.

It had been a couple months since Carrie's heart attack. Everyone had loved his idea of a welcome home party. Now he wondered if he'd taken on more than he could handle.

Noah glanced around the kitchen. Carrie's knickknacks stared back at him.

"Noah, you are doing great." Ian Richards patted his ample belly, and leaned against the kitchen entryway.

Sardines in a can. Noah bit his lip as the big guy he lovingly called "Big Bro" seemed to fill up the space.

"You need to relax, little bro."

Noah glanced up into Ian's sweet round face and brown eyes. A face that made Noah feel safe and happy. "I'm trying."

"Deep breaths. Just like I taught you. You got this, bro."

Noah closed his eyes and took a couple of deep breaths. Although he was doing this more for Ian than himself, it did help him feel better. At least it gave the illusion he was at peace.

"Got the ladder," said a voice.

"Be careful with that thing in here." Noah moved quickly to help the new arrival. "If Grammy Carrie's knickknacks get broken, she'll be pissed."

Rick Danvers was half a foot taller than Noah, with black-gray hair. He wore a flannel shirt and jeans. Rick had been one of Daddy Mason's farm hands since long before they came to the farm a few years back.

"Get that thing out of here." Noah pointed back out of the kitchen. "You guys can use the chairs to stand on and hang the banner."

Rick sighed. "Okay, Brandon, take it back."

"You got it," came a disembodied voice.

Brandon?!

Noah felt his face fill with heat and quickly busied himself with the fridge. He called out from behind the door. "Ian, you think I should make up the punch now, or should I wait?"

Instead of a response, Ian chuckled. "Why is your face so red, Noah? Are you okay?"

"I'm fine."

"Uh-huh." Ian chuckled and pulled out a folded banner from a manila envelope. "I got the banner back from the printers."

"Great." Noah pulled out the meat tray from the fridge. He then carefully removed the cover. "As soon as Brandon and Rick finish fooling around with the ladder, have them put it up."

As if on cue, Rick and Brandon returned. Brandon turned a char and stepped onto it.

Brandon Carsey was half a foot taller than Noah, without the added height of the furniture. From this angle, one of

Brandon's most attractive parts was staring Noah in the face. Or was he staring at it?

When Brandon looked down to take the end of the banner from Ian, Noah quickly ducked behind the fridge door again to hide the fact he had been looking. From that safe spot, he admired the rest of Brandon. His face was the shape of an upside-down teardrop. His blondish-brown hair was shaved along three sides, with the top slightly longer and brushed to one side. His jeans hung a little loose but hinted at the muscle tone that made Noah's blood boil.

There was never any doubt that Brandon had cared deeply for Noah since they met. They'd even gone on one date, but Noah had ruined it with his nerves. He hated the fact that he was too broken to be loved. *No, stop it.* Mason and Ian loved him dearly, or, as they had said on many occasions, he wouldn't be there with them right now.

Brandon took several thumbtacks and put them between his teeth. Ian handed Rick the other end of the banner, and he took a chair to the other side of the kitchen. Upon unfolding the whole thing, the sign read, "Welcome Home, Grammy."

Noah's skin was crawling. Was Grammy Carrie going to be upset that they had done all this for her? Would she be okay with her bridge friends seeing her right out of the hospital? A hundred worries chased each other through his mind.

"I can't wait to see Mrs. Dale again," Rick commented. "I mean, Carrie."

Noah couldn't help but smile. It was pretty obvious also that Rick had feelings for Grammy Carrie. He even took her to dinner once—the night of her heart attack. The thought sent a chill down Noah's spine. He had been so scared. Ian and

Rick had been terrific. Both acted quickly with the call to the ambulance and getting her to the hospital and of course, the several panicked calls to Daddy Mason.

He had to get his thoughts in order and his mind off the past. Grammy Carrie had recovered and was on her way home.

"Hold it still," Ian started walking around Rick.

"Mmmm. IT thhhhhhr," Brandon mumbled, trying to pinpoint a spot for Rick to pin the banner.

Without missing a beat, Ian gently smacked Brandon on the leg. "Hush you. Don't talk with your mouth full."

"That's what he said." Noah got out of his head just long enough to give the obvious one-liner. Everyone in the kitchen, save Brandon, busted up laughing. He just shot Noah a disquieted look, and instantly Noah began to regret commenting. Had Brandon gotten offended by the joke? *Damn.*

Brandon just growled and finished tacking up the banner.

Noah turned his attention to the fridge and was about to remove the lemon-lime soda when a vibrating phone stopped them.

"Awww, crap!"

Noah looked over at Ian. "What's wrong?"

"Daddy Mason and Carrie are going to be delayed. They are stopping to pick up the new farmhand." Ian put his phone facedown on the table.

Noah looked up at the ceiling and let out a sigh.

Brandon and Rick had just finished hanging the banner.

Noah started to worry. Should he call Carrie's bridge ladies and tell them there'd been a delay for the welcome home party? Were any of them even going to show up?

"Now what?" Brandon finally removed his jeans-clad package from eye level by stepping down from the chair.

"Put the cold stuff back in the fridge and wait." Noah started to cover the meat and cheese tray. "I guess," he finished under his breath.

"Here, I'll help." Brandon covered the chocolate chip cookies and handed the tray to Noah, who turned and put it in the fridge.

"Hey guys, did you hear that?" Ian held up his hand for silence. "It sounds like a car pulling up."

Noah raised his eyebrow and shook his head. "I don't hear..." Before he could finish his sentence, a car door slammed shut. "Who could that be? Is it one of the ladies Grammy plays bridge with?"

"Well, little bro, only one way to find out." Ian motioned for Noah to join him.

"I'll go." Brandon moved to the door and stepped out, letting the screen door bang shut behind him.

The noise startled Noah momentarily. His knuckles turned white as he clutched the door handle on the fridge.

Should he pull everything out again? Was this one of the ladies? He had called and invited them. Where was Brandon? He seemed to be taking a long time to find out who was here.

Almost as if on cue, Brandon returned. His eyes were wide.

"Who's here?" Rick stepped forward.

"Some lady is looking for Noah." Brandon shot Noah a surprised look and shrugged his shoulders.

"Me?" The hair on the back of Noah's neck stood on end. "It's probably one of the ladies Grammy plays bridge with each week. I'll go find out. Ian, will you please come with me in case they brought anything to be carried in?"

"Sure," Ian followed Noah out the kitchen door.

The moment Noah stepped out on the porch, he heard his name. And his blood ran cold.

Mother!

She had found him. This was not good. Despite the warm autumn weather, she was dressed in a long-sleeve white blouse and jeans. Her long brown hair had been pulled back in a ponytail, and her eyes looked red from crying. But this was her, Kelly Easton. The woman who gave him life.

"Do you know this lady, Noah?"

Noah's mother took a step forward and reached out for him. Panic seized him, and he stepped back, nearly colliding with Ian's ample belly. "No." Noah put up his hand to stop her approach. "Stay there."

"Who is she?" Ian asked again.

"Kelly Easton. The woman who gave birth to me."

"Is this your friend Mason?" Her voice grated on Noah's nerves.

"No, Kelly, this is Ian. What do you want?" *Damn, why did I give her his name?*

Kelly ran the side of her finger under one eye. It was clear she still was crying. Noah could start to feel his eyes burn and become blurred with liquid rage.

"Noah, please, I don't want any trouble. I just need to talk to you. It's important."

"How did you even find me?"

"I was the nurse who cared for Carrie Dale during her recovery. I took a chance that the Noah she talked about and thought so highly of was my son."

Noah cringed. Grammy? Did she know Kelly was his mother? What was so crucial that Kelly had to come looking for him? Surely it couldn't be that important. Where the hell was she when he struggled for food and shelter for years on the street? Where was she when his father was constantly beating and harassing him? Why didn't she protect him, like a mother was supposed to do for her children?

Thoughts of his biological father and his life before the streets sent an old fire burning through his system. "Where the hell were you?" Noah let his rage blast out at her. "Where the fuck were you when I was begging for scraps on the street? When I came close to selling myself for a bite to eat and temporary shelter? A mother is supposed to protect and care for her children!"

"Noah, please. I was not in a good place. After your father went to prison, I tried to find you. I tried as hard as I could to find you." Kelly wiped her eyes again.

"You obviously didn't try hard enough."

At that point, Kelly took a step forward. "I am sorry, Noah."

Noah took a step back, pressing himself against Ian, and Noah felt his friend's arms encircle him, but he shrugged them off. He took a step toward his mother. "Sorry? You are sorry? Fuck you, Kelly. Just leave... Now."

Kelly stood her ground. She took a deep breath and looked away from him.

"Fine! You said you wanted to tell me something. Tell me and be gone. I've learned to live without you, and I don't need you now."

"I came to tell you…your father was released from prison three weeks ago. He's in Remington City and has been for the last two weeks."

"Why should I believe you?"

"Despite all our issues, I don't want to see you get hurt anymore."

"So *now* you want to protect me?" His scorn flew from his mouth with deadly venom.

"I tried several…" She glanced up at Ian resentfully and then back at Noah. "Can we please talk in private?"

"No. Anything you say to me, you can say in front of Ian. He's my witness if you try anything."

"Look, I only want to get to know my son and warn him he could be in danger. I don't mean any harm. Please, don't you see that?"

"The only thing I see is that I have a good-for-nothing mother who ran like a scared chicken when daddy made a fist!"

That seemed to burn the woman. She took a couple of steps back and lowered her head. "I…I guess I deserved that."

"Noah, your mother…" Ian stepped forward.

"That woman gave birth to me. She is not my mother." Noah turned to face the house and pointed. "Carrie has been more of a fucking mother to me than that woman."

"I love you, Noah. I'm not going to give up on you. You will see me again. I will try to make things right with you if it's the last thing I do."

"I wish you luck, because I will always hate you. Do you hear me? I hate you!" Noah wiped the stinging liquid from his eyes.

"Fine." She turned to open her car door. "I'll leave for now, but I will be back."

He laughed viciously as she climbed into her car and took off down the drive.

He let out a flood of emotion the minute her car was out of sight. He covered his eyes with his hands and began to sob.

How dare she? How dare she come looking for him now? *Where the hell has she been for the last five years?*

This time, Ian put his arms around Noah again and held him. Noah melted into Ian's warm, soft embrace. One of the few places Noah ever felt safe.

"Shh, little bro. It's alright. It's going to be alright."

Ian's cooing was as gentle as the sweet song of a nightingale. Noah was starting to feel better. The counselor at the center had told him a good cry was soul cleansing and overdue. And a good cry was what he needed. How many years ago had it been since that kind therapist tried to help him? Three years? Two? It was hard to determine anymore how much that man had helped. What was his name? Mike? Jake? Matt? Something like that.

It didn't matter. I have Mason and Ian now. My bear family. And now thanks to them, and now Caleb, Luke, and Drake. Like one big family.

"Noah, Ian, everything all..." Brandon stepped out on the porch.

Noah looked up into Brandon's wide eyes.

Chapter Two

"Am I interrupting something?" Brandon just stared at Noah and Ian.

"No, not interrupting. Noah just got a little emotional." Ian patted Noah's back.

Noah let go of Ian and turned to face Brandon. "Would you like to go for a walk, and I'll explain?"

Brandon looked at Ian, who nodded. Then back at Noah. "Sure."

Brandon motioned for Noah to take the lead. Noah smiled faintly. The beard Noah worked so hard to grow in the last couple of months bunched in the corner of his mouth. His slim dancer's body was draped in loose jeans and T-shirt.

"Brandon, try to be back before Mason and Grammy. They have the new farmhand with them. And don't forget about the welcome home party."

Brandon nodded at Ian and started to follow Noah off the porch.

Ian grabbed for his arm and whispered sternly into his ear. "Be kind to him. He just had a bad ordeal."

Brandon nodded. "Understood." While a jolly fellow most of the time, Ian tended to intimidate him due to his size.

Brandon knew that Noah was sleeping with both Ian and Mason. They had some strange relationships based on a family format. Despite that, he had always been attracted to Noah. Ever since that night at the Rainbow Rose when Noah drunkenly kissed him.

"Let's head towards the trees." Noah pointed to a path behind the house that led to a small patch of trees.

"I have a question for you." Brandon put a hand gently on Noah's arm. "Who was that woman?"

"The woman who gave birth to me."

"Your mother?"

"Kelly Easton is many things, but being a mother is not her strong suit. She's a coward and a bitch."

Brandon's jaw fell open. He had always prided himself on having a good relationship with his parents. It was amazing for him to hear Noah spew this anger and hurt outright. It would probably be best to change the subject. If Noah wanted to talk more about her, he would.

"Daddy Mason has been more of a parent to me than my biological parents."

Brandon leaped on the moment and asked, "So you and Mason are dating?" He felt his heart sink a little lower into his stomach.

"No, Mason is my daddy dom."

"To me, that denotes a romantic relationship."

"Not in our case." Noah leaned his back against a tree. "Mason has a primary. Caleb Olivera. You met him that night in the hospital when we were there for Grammy Carrie."

"Oh, yes. The businessman you and Ian were trying to set him up with a couple of months ago. How is that going?"

"That's right, and good so far."

"So, you guys still fool around?" Brandon lowered his eyebrows.

"Sometimes. Daddy James, Mason's late husband, used to say that sex was a great tool for strengthening and building bonds."

This wasn't helping Brandon's nerves any. Was Noah single, or wasn't he? This didn't have to be that complicated, did it? "What about Ian? You two are practically inseparable."

Noah smiled. "He's also Mason's cub."

"So, that means..."

Noah stepped away from the tree. "In a nutshell, it means that we are three close friends who occasionally fool around with each other." Noah smiled wickedly as if picking up on Brandon's slight discomfort. After a brief moment, he continued, "And no, I don't have a primary or what you would call a boyfriend. Technically, I'm single."

Brandon almost let out a sigh of relief, but he wanted to play it cool for Noah.

They continued to walk farther into the wooded area. Eventually, Noah leaned against another tree. He looked back towards the house, far in the distance.

Brandon reached out a hand and ran his open palm along Noah's soft golden beard. "You know..." He paused briefly. "I never forgot that kiss at the club several months back."

Noah broke eye contact. "Oh, that. I was drunk."

"So was I."

After a short awkward pause, Brandon stepped forward. "Wouldn't mind it was happening again."

This time, Noah's eyes sparkled. Each damn time Brandon wanted to reach out to Noah, something had always gotten in the way. Not this time. This time it was just him and Noah, out in the trees, no one around.

Brandon slid a hand gently against Noah's cheek and pressed himself up against Noah, lodging one leg between his knees.

Noah closed his eyes and raised his lips, anticipating.

Brandon lowered his own onto Noah's, gently forcing Noah's mouth open. Brandon could taste the chocolate chip cookies Noah had munched on earlier. He felt Noah's arms circle his waist. As the kiss deepened, Noah started lowering himself to the ground, and to keep the kiss going, Brandon followed.

Brandon lay on his back, and Noah rested his head on Brandon's chest. Words were not needed at this point.

Would anything ever become of this? What was going on between him and Noah anyway?

Brandon started gently rubbing Noah's back, and Noah snuggled into him.

There were feelings here, but how would Brandon help bring them to the surface? With all the hurt and trauma in Noah's way, he may never be able to have a stable relationship. But would he be here with Brandon now if that was the case?

Brandon closed his eyes and just tried to live in the moment. A moment that may not come again.

The sun was warm. Birds sang a sweet love song as if they approved the intimate scene playing in the woods.

Brandon let out a sigh. "Is this okay?"

Noah nodded. "Yes."

"This is nice." Brandon put his arm around Noah's slight frame. "I wish we could have many more moments like this one."

The words must have been the wrong thing to say. Noah froze in Brandon's arms.

"I mean…"

Noah started struggling to pull free. "No, please let go."

"What? Did I say something wrong?"

"No, you didn't. I just…" Noah closed his eyes and bit his lip. After a moment, he opened them again. "I just can't. I'm sorry." Tears started streaming down his face, and before Brandon could stop him, he ran back down the path.

Fuck! Brandon jumped to his feet and started after him.

"Noah, wait. I'm sorry." *Fuck, what the hell just happened?*

Noah sped up, reaching the porch first greeting Carrie as she stepped out of the truck. Her long blond hair pulled back in a ponytail and she wore a white sundress.

"How are you doing?" he asked Carrie.

"Doing a lot better."

Mason and an older gentleman with brownish-gray hair and a five o'clock shadow shook hands.

Mason Dale was a tall man with muscles and tone to spare. His gentle brown eyes turned to Noah as Brandon reached the porch. "Hey Noah, Brandon. I would like you to meet Mark Jennings. Mark, this is my adopted boy Noah and fellow farmhand Brandon Carsey."

Noah took a step backward. His eyes were wide and darting back and forth.

Brandon glanced at Noah. What's wrong with him? He looked terrified. He returned his attention to Mark Jennings, holding out his hand "Hello. A pleasure to meet you. You'll like it here."

"I hope so." Mark's handshake was firm as he took Brandon's hand. Mark turned to Noah. "Hello, Noah. Good to see you again. Is this where you've been hiding these days?"

Noah didn't answer him but locked his gaze on the ground. "Yes, sir," he mumbled.

"You two know each other...," Mason motioned his hand between Mark and Noah.

"Yeah, we're old friends. Right, Noah?"

Something in Mark's voice sent Brandon's nerves on edge. His infliction of "old" may have had something to do with it.

Without looking up, Noah nodded and mumbled another, "Yes, sir."

What was this reaction? Was Noah that shook up about himself and Brandon? What was it with this newcomer? It wasn't like Noah to act like this. How did Mark and Noah know each other? Noah seemed almost what? Terrified? Why? Brandon's gaze went from Mark to Noah and back again. No, it was him. It's this man. He's the reason Noah went quiet. Who was he, and how did they know each other?

"If you'll excuse me, everyone, I'll go lie down. I'm not feeling well." Noah moved to enter the house. He slipped in through the door and disappeared inside.

"Noah... And he's gone." Brandon moved to follow Noah, but Mason put his hand out to block his path.

"I need you to take Mark to the bunkhouse so he can settle in." Mason motioned to the bunkhouse, where Brandon and Rick slept.

"But, I... Noah... He..."

"He what?" Mason's face twisted into a mask of irritability. He folded his arms across his chest.

Brandon sighed. He would have to talk to Noah later and find out what happened and the issue with the new farmhand. Guess the welcome home party is off for now. Maybe after Noah calmed down a little bit.

"Alright, boss." Brandon pointed to the suitcases sitting on the porch. "Grab your gear and follow me."

"Great." Mark grabbed his suitcases and other items.

What was Noah's connection to this man? He hardly seemed happy to see Mark. It was apparent that they weren't as close friends as Mark tried to lead Brandon and Mason to believe. Noah seemed terrified of the man. More than his general fear of strangers. That was not like him at all.

Well, work beckoned. He would have to talk it over with Noah later.

Brandon led Mark down the path to the bunkhouse, which sat about fifteen feet from the barn. The bunkhouse was a small cabin-like house with room for three people to sleep comfortably, with a bathroom and kitchen. Not that the kitchen got much use, as Mrs. Dale always expected everyone to eat together in the kitchen for all meals.

Mrs. Dale was always happiest when everyone on the farm was gathered together in her kitchen—despite it barely being big enough to fit everyone. It would be interesting to see how she would pull this off with an extra body to feed. Brandon chuckled silently as he reached the door of the bunk house. He knocked once and opened the door. The place was deserted. Rick must be out doing something somewhere else on the farm.

"This is the bunkhouse. There are three bedrooms, a bathroom, and a kitchen. However, the kitchen doesn't get much use. We all generally eat at the main house for all our meals. Mrs. Dale doesn't know how to cook small meals."

Mark nodded. "Understandable." He looked around the small cabin. "Where will I be sleeping?"

"Well, this room is mine." Brandon pointed to his and Rick's rooms and then the third room, which had a curtain for a door rather than a solid door. "You will be in here." Brandon took a deep breath and let it out slowly.

Mason had been discussing getting an extra set of hands on the farm after his mother's heart attack. Noah and Ian had mostly taken over the household chores, feeding the chickens and gardening, or at least helping with the gardening. There were several things that Mrs. Dale insisted on still doing, and that was one of them. She never trusted anyone in her garden.

Mark moved his stuff into his room and drew the curtain closed, muttering something like thank you to Brandon as he passed by.

Well, at least Rick would have someone near his age to talk to and wouldn't have to be bored talking with Brandon.

Brandon signed and turned his attention to his room. He entered and closed the door, still wondering what had happened with Noah earlier. Brandon's room was loosely decorated with a couple of sports team pennants. Mostly baseball-one local, and one Major League team. Several baseball trophies were sitting on the small dresser in the far corner, along with a twin-size bed with a slightly uncomfortable mattress.

Brandon collapsed on the bed and tucked his hands behind his head. Noah was a complicated man. At twenty-four years old, Noah had a complicated life. First, he'd survived a domestic violence situation, and then lived on the streets.

Brandon thought back to the first time he met Noah. Mason, Noah, and Ian had just come to the farm after Ethan Dale's passing. Brandon was taken aback by Noah almost immediately. His short frame. His gentle, compassionate nature. It didn't take long for Brandon to realize that Noah had been seriously traumatized.

They interacted well over the year or so that they had been on the farm. Brandon remembered when he had tried to ask Noah out on a date and how the date turned out. It had been a nightmare for Noah. He kept looking around and acting like the large groups of people at the theater and restaurant were going to hurt him. Noah had to sit with the wall at his back. It was almost as if the boy was terrified of his own shadow.

Mason had told him that Noah came from a troubled home.

Brandon sighed and turned to lie on his side. He knew there were feelings there. He wished he knew how to help Noah bring them to the surface. Something was standing in the way of it. Perhaps whatever traumatized Noah in the past was what's blocking his feelings for Brandon now. If only there were a way to get past it.

Soon there was a knock on the door. "Hey man, do you need to use the restroom? I'm going to take a shower." Mark's voice rang into the room. Damn, if the sound of that man's voice didn't set Brandon's nerves on edge. What was it about that man that he didn't like? It couldn't just be his voice.

"No, I'm good. Help yourself."

"Thanks, man."

"No problem."

Well, he could pretty well take care of himself from here on out. Best to get back to work and deal with his feelings for Noah another time. Brandon stood up and headed out.

Chapter Three

Noah wiped his eyes as he entered the room he shared with Ian and closed the door. He didn't feel like having the damned party now after the day that he had had.

First his mother, now his damned sperm donor. Shit. He couldn't stay here with that man. Okay, exit strategy. Wasn't anything different than before? Being here was no different than any other place that Noah had to move away from in his life.

Noah had gotten so attached to Mason, James, and Ian. Even after James's death and later Carrie's heart attack and near death, he was starting to feel like he was just going to keep losing or nearly losing people who had been so kind and gentle to him. She was more like a mother to him than Kelly fucking Easton. How in the hell was he going to be able to leave without making a commotion? Did Mason know he had hired Noah's father as a new farmhand? No, if he had known, he wouldn't have hired him. But then, how was he to know? Noah knew right now that he had to find a way to leave without causing a commotion.

Somehow, he had to leave and get away from Mark. There was no point in telling Daddy Mason, Grammy Carrie, or Ian. He'd just spent too much time here. He'd gotten too close. Damn James for his kind heart. Why did he have to believe that this would be different finally? Nothing had changed. Noah had started to believe that maybe it would be different. The Dale family had been more of a family to Noah than his real family, and he had grown to love them so much. Ian, his adopted brother, was not a member of the Dale family but had become more like family than Noah would ever have liked to admit. Ian was so kind and gentle, and it was easy to believe Ian and Daddy Mason could protect him from anything. But they couldn't protect him from the father who had such control over him.

It's not control. It's fear.

"Noah?" Ian's voice sounded muffled from the other side of the door. They had both agreed that even though they shared the room, if one was inside and the door was closed, they would still knock to announce their presence on the off chance the other wanted some alone time.

"It's open." Noah quickly tried to dry his tears. The last thing he needed was Ian seeing him crying again.

The door swung open, and Ian stepped into the room. "Daddy Mason wants to make sure your chores are finished before din..." He stopped midsentence. "Are you okay, little bro?"

"No." Noah fell onto his bed. A heavy sigh escaped his lips. "Kelly's visit upset me more than I realized."

It wasn't a lie, but then again, skirting or omitting the truth was something Noah had gotten good at over the years. And how in the hell was he supposed to tell Ian that the man Daddy Mason hired was the abusive asshole who beat him twice a month for most of his life?

The point was, he couldn't. No matter how much he thought Ian or Mason would be able to help, neither of them knew what they would be up against in this particular situation. Mark was very good at coming up with ways to torture Noah. When it came to forms of abuse, the man had turned it into an art form. That man was a monster, and a very clever damn monster at that.

"Little bro." Ian sat down beside Noah. "Listen to me. Your mom meant well, She-"

Noah cut him off before he could continue. "Kelly Easton is not my mother. She's a coward and a bitch."

"Yeah, but that cowardly bitch took a chance to warn you and try to reconnect. I mean, that showed some real guts."

"Well, I appreciate the warning, but I still hate her guts. She got to get on with her life, go to school, become a nurse, while I was fucking suffering on the streets and trying to find scraps to eat."

"Well, think of it this way. You would never have found us otherwise."

Noah sighed. Ian was right. Had he not tried pickpocketing James on the street corner, he would never have met Mason or Ian.

"I'm sorry, little bro."

"For what?" Noah sat up, looking at Ian with a doubtful eyebrow.

"It's the one who hates who hurts worse than the hated."

Noah sighed heavier and fell back on the bed. Ian was right again. Damn him for being so wise. And damn right, he hurt worse. While he was struggling on the street, Kelly, his so-called mother, was getting to do everything she always wanted to do. She went back to school to become a nurse. Grammy wouldn't be here if not for her.

Noah always wanted an everyday life like his classmates at school. How come she got one when his own life had been ruined? Noah sat up. "I'm going to go do my chores. I'll catch you later, big bro."

Noah gave Ian a big hug. "Thank you for the talk. I'll think about what you said."

He left the room and headed down to the barn.

He'd stayed too long, he thought again to himself. He should never have gotten involved with James Dale. Now he was stuck, and at the most crucial moment, he needed to leave them. It was the only way he could protect them from that monster. They were too close, and someone was going to get hurt.

"Hiya, Noah."

Noah looked up as he entered the barn. Rick carried a bale of hay on hooks.

"Hi, Rick." After a moment, he asked, "Where's that new guy?"

"Mason sent him and Brandon to help Grammy in her garden. They should be back soon."

"Oh. But we planned a welcome home party for her."

"Is everything alright?"

"Yes, everything is fine."

"Mark says he's a friend of yours."

That's an overstatement if Noah ever heard one before. "Yeah. I knew him before Mason and Ian."

"I see. What do you know about him?" Rick slammed down the bale of hay.

Noah ignored the question and quickly asked, "How's your son doing? The one my age?"

"He's doing well." Rick used a small pocketknife to cut open the hay bale, and the bundle disintegrated into a pile. "He just started his second year of med school, and..." After a short pause, he asked, "Noah, you sure you're okay?"

"Yes, I'm fine. I don't want to talk about Mark. If that's alright with you."

"Why? Did he do something to you way back when?"

"No, I just don't know him all that well," Noah answered, probably a little too quickly. After a moment, he changed the subject. "You must be proud of him. And why not? Medical school is a big deal. I wish I could have gone to college." He grabbed a pair of gloves hanging on a nearby wall.

"It's never too late, you know. You are still young." Rick did a quick look around. "Damn, we only have one pitchfork."

Noah did the same thing. Rick was right. There was only one. "I think Brandon had one near the tack room, but I'm not sure."

"Why don't you use this one, and I'll fetch the other?" Rick motioned to the one next to him.

Noah nodded and took it. As Rick started away, Noah began to pitch hay into the cow troughs.

What would his life have been like if he had gone to college? Would he be graduating by now? How much easier life would have been?

Resentfully, Noah filled the first trough and moved on to the second.

"So, this is where you been hiding out all these years."

Noah's blood ran cold, and he turned to face Mark Easton. The face that had haunted his nightmares for years.

Quickly, Noah's gaze locked to the floor. "Please, no." Noah dropped the pitchfork and tried to exit the barn, but Mark blocked his path with his muscular frame. "No, I don't think so."

"Why are you here? Why can't you leave me alone?" Noah raised his voice.

"Shhhh. Do you want the others to hear you?"

"You shouldn't be here. I have a restraining order against you."

"You think a piece of paper can stop your father?"

Noah took several steps backward. He remembered how he left that final day and how the police had arrested Mark. By that point, Kelly was long gone, and the bitch never thought to take Noah with her. Noah had to fight it out on the streets because he was of age and didn't have a job. He had to leave the house that had meant so much terror to him.

"You are a-"

"Careful, Noah. I hate to have to remove my belt." He smiled evilly.

"We're both here. Great. Maybe I can pay you back for those years of my life you took."

What did he mean by that? He couldn't possibly believe that his getting arrested was Noah's fault. Noah wasn't the one who called the police during one of their sprawls on the front lawn. Several of the neighbors saw Mark whipping Noah. Any one of them could have called the police, but boy had he been thankful it was finally over. The man was clearly insane.

"You did all this to yourself. If you didn't beat Kelly or me, we'd..."

"Be what, Noah? One big happy family? You're pathetic. You know I was trying to make you a man."

Mark's sinister snicker sent revulsion rolling through Noah's stomach. "A man? How can a coward make a boy into a man?"

Mark's nostrils flared. Time for a quick retreat.

Noah took a couple of steps backward. "You stay the fuck away from me."

Mark stepped forward, almost in Noah's face. "Or you'll what?" He reached up and smacked Noah gently on the cheek. "Come on, big man, do something." He repeated the gesture.

Noah moved farther back. "I said fucking stop!"

"Only men, older men, get to tell other men what to do, Noah. Not boys who get fucked in the ass."

"You're disgusting!" Noah spoke through his gritted teeth.

"I'll be watching you, boy, and when you least expect it... Bam!" Mark faked a punch, making Noah flinch. "One fist for every year in the slammer."

Noah's mind was racing. His emotions were floating around him: fear, resentment, anger, and other emotions pooled in his eyes.

"No, no, the difference is country music has too much of a..."

At the sound of Brandon's voice, Noah looked up. He and Rick were walking into the barn.

Thank God. Thank fucking God.

The moment Mark was distracted, Noah took off. He had to get away from Mark and away from Dale Farm. As long as Mark was there, he would never be safe. But how?

"Noah, are you alright?" Brandon's words seemed lost in the wind. "Noah..."

He had to get away from Mark, away from the barn.

All he could think of was the safety of his room. But what would stop Mark from entering the house and following through with this threat?

As he moved quickly away, memories invaded his mind. That last night was the worst. The bruises, the sprained wrist, and injured arm after he tried to use it to defend himself against his father's belt.

Even after Noah's father was incarcerated, the social workers tried to help him, but things weren't going to work. He was free but on his own. Noah tried hard to find a job but couldn't. He had no skills he could sell.

No, he couldn't stay where Mark was. But Grammy Carrie had just had a heart attack, and Daddy Mason didn't hang out all day at the house. Especially now, since he was seeing Caleb Olivera.

"Noah, wipe your feet." Grammy Carrie called as he entered the house. He didn't pay much attention as he fled to his room and closed the door. Overwhelmed, he collapsed on the bed for a good cry.

Chapter Four

Brandon had just reached the porch when Carrie Dale stepped out the kitchen door, blocking his path. "Whoa, there, slick."

"Mrs. Dale, I…"

The sixty-some-year-old woman held up a hand. "No. Noah's pretty upset. Did something happen?"

"That's what I'm trying to find out."

"Noah was pretty upset when he came flying in here. Probably a good idea to let him be for the rest of the day."

"But, I…"

"No buts. Get back to work. When Noah's ready to talk, he will."

Brandon let out a heavy sigh. She was right. Noah needed some time to calm down and relax. "Alright, Mrs. Dale. Please let him know I'll be in the barn if he wants to talk later."

Carrie nodded and headed to the porch swing.

Brandon headed off to the barn. When he got there, Rick and Mark were working together, feeding the cows. Rick was heaving small batches of hay into the troughs. Mark stood with his hand on the top of his pitchfork handle, resting his chin on the back of his gloved hand.

"Maybe later on tonight we could go out for a beer." Mark glanced up at Brandon as he approached. "You'd be welcome to come too if you want."

"There's a great bar on Twenty-First Street I've wanted to visit. It's an old-fashioned honky tonk." Rick pointed at Brandon. "Maybe Noah would like to go too?"

"I don't think I wanna go out tonight. And I know Noah's not in a good place. Being in a crowded bar would not be good for him."

"That's too bad. I hope my old friend gets feeling better." Mark's face twisted into a mask of concern, but something in the tone of Mark's voice alerted Brandon that he was hoping for the opposite. What was this strange connection between Mark and Noah?

Mark pulled off his gloves. "I need some water. Could you guys finish up?"

Rick glared at Mark for a brief moment before he nodded.

Mark handed the gloves and the pitchfork to Brandon "Thanks, guys." He exited the barn.

"What's his problem?" Brandon slid on the gloves.

"Beats the fuck outta me." Rick stopped for a moment. "How's Noah? Is he okay?"

Brandon shrugged. "I don't know." Maybe he could talk to Rick about what was bothering him. Rick was older and wiser. "To be honest, I'm a little confused."

Rick leaned the pitchfork against the wall and removed his gloves. "How so?"

"I don't know how to explain it."

"Try."

"It's Noah. Whenever I feel we're getting close, he pulls away and runs off. Like today on our walk. It was almost like he's afraid of his feelings."

Rick raised his eyebrows in astonishment. "I can see how that can be frustrating." After a brief pause, he continued, "From what I understand, he's had a tough life. It's rather colored his opinions of things, especially relationships. I sympathize with you, but you have to..." Rick looked up for a moment, "Give him some time... or not."

Confused, Brandon muttered, "What?"

Rick lifted his outstretched hand.

Brandon turned to see Noah leaning against the door with his arms crossed. Shit! How much had he heard? "Hi, Noah. Are you feeling better?"

"I'll let you guys talk." Rick left the barn, closing the barn door behind him.

Noah stepped forward, uncrossing his arms. "I'm sorry about earlier."

Brandon nodded. "Apology accepted."

"Thank you." Noah smiled weakly and looked at the ground. "It wasn't you that upset me."

"I was worried I had."

"I know. Grammy told me."

"Mrs. Dale?"

"I call her Grammy because she's Daddy Mason's mother."

Brandon nodded. He still didn't quite understand how this whole poly thing worked that connected Mason, Noah, and Ian. But he was willing to learn more about it for Noah.

An awkward silence filled the air. Noah glanced up at Brandon and then back at his feet.

"No, Noah, you don't have to look at the ground. Look at me." Brandon hooked his index finger and raised Noah's chin gently.

Noah locked eyes with him briefly before looking away. "I'm sorry."

"Don't be sorry. Do you know how much I've come to care about you? You know that, right?"

"I do."

Brandon took a step closer. "I would like to explore these feelings more."

"Oh, Brandon, I..." Noah paused. He glanced up at Brandon with those radiant eyes. "I'm too broken to be loved."

"That's not true. You are a good, caring, and loving man. I know you have feelings for me." Brandon moved another step closer. "Don't you?"

"I don't know."

Brandon reached out carefully and brushed the back of his hand along Noah's cheek. "It's okay if you don't know. I have enough for both of us to share."

He pulled Noah into a kiss.

Noah moaned as his hands found their way under Brandon's shirt.

Noah murmured something that almost sounded like "what a nice distraction, fuck that bastard."

The contact of Noah's hands started a chain reaction of warm and tingly sensations soaring through Brandon.

Noah deepened the kiss, trying to pull Brandon closer, pressing his smaller body against Brandon.

Keeping the kiss going, Brandon walked backward to the pile of hay. He gently guided Noah down onto him.

Noah fell onto his hands and knees before laying his weight on Brandon. Brandon sat up as Noah began tugging at his shirt, unable to pull it off. Noah looked frustrated and about ready to give up, when Brandon pulled off his shirt, exposing his bare, flat, hairy chest to Noah.

Noah's fingers ran through that chest hair. Brandon moaned and slipped his hands up Noah's back. If he was going to be shirtless, then Noah would have to be too.

Noah must have sensed Brandon's thoughts because he let Brandon pull off his shirt. As soon as the smaller man's was bare, Brandon ran his fingertips down the slow trail of his body, and Noah sighed with pleasure. The sound was like primal music. He wanted to ask Noah if he was okay with this, but a sudden fear followed the thought. If he asked, would it break the spell? Would Noah rush to get his shirt on and run back for the house's safety?

You need to show Noah that you are a haven too.

Brandon braced his hands on the small of Noah's back, and Noah started kissing the side of Brandon's face, down the side of his neck, along his shoulder, and pec, but when he reached Brandon's nipple, he sucked it hungrily into his mouth.

The sudden shock made Brandon arch his body up. He cupped the back of Noah's head as Noah's tongue lapped at the small nub, sending an electrical shock through him. He arched a little and groaned out.

Every nerve was on fire, by the time Noah started moving his kisses farther down Brandon's chest and stomach. He stopped to trace the ridges of Brandon's four-pack abs with the tip of his tongue. He continued until he reached the waistband of Brandon's jeans. He looked up at Brandon, a question blaring in his eyes.

Unable to find words, Brandon just nodded. Words seemed useless at this point.

Carefully, Noah unfastened Brandon's jeans and tried pulling them down. Brandon shifted one hip and then the other to help Noah remove them. Brandon was startled by the momentary exposure as his prick bounced out almost fully erect.

Noah only pulled Brandon's jeans and underwear to his knees and laid them on top, trapping Brandon in place.

Noah's tongue danced around the head of Brandon's tool.

Let him have all he wants. Let him see how much you love him and how much you are willing to do to be his.

Maybe this was what was needed. Noah needed to feel safe and... Before Brandon could finish his thought, Noah's mouth engulfed him, long and deep. The sensation wiped all thoughts from Brandon's mind like the wiping of a chalkboard.

God fucking damn, that felt good. The dude had had some practice. Fuck!

Brandon dropped the thought as Noah kept working his lips over Brandon's prick.

After several moments, Noah stood and removed his jeans.

Brandon quickly shot out a hand and took hold of Noah's wrist. "Are you sure? We don't have to."

Noah bit his lip and nodded. "I want to. Please?"

He had given Noah his out, and Noah didn't want to take it. Noah did have feelings for him. If only he could show Noah that he didn't have to be afraid of them.

Brandon nodded and lowered his head onto the hay. He raised it as Noah stood straddling him. Then Noah lowered himself. He took hold of Noah's hips to guide him slowly down into place. He had no problem letting Noah know he was in control. He wanted Noah to know that Brandon was a safe place. A place he didn't need to fear. He tried to convey this with his eyes.

Brandon ran his hands across Noah's chest as Noah began rising, then lowering, over and over as he rode Brandon's shaft.

Every instinct pushed Brandon to begin thrusting his hips, but he refrained with every ounce of his being. Noah was in charge, and he refused to take it back. He wanted Noah to enjoy the feeling of being in control.

Brandon covered the top of Noah's prick with his hand, forcing it to rub against his furry belly and calloused palm. A loud, primal grunt escaped from Noah's lips. Noah moaned louder, becoming wilder in his up and down dance on Brandon's cock. Each time was pushing Brandon into a more primitive state. Thought was becoming impossible. Brandon slowly started thrusting his hips up to meet Noah. Very slow and gentle at first.

Noah's eyes rolled back into his head, which also rolled back. "My God, Brandon" escaped from his lips.

Soon, Brandon began to feel the build-up in pressure. If things continued, he would blow his load deep inside Noah.

Just as Brandon came to that conclusion, Noah let out a loud, "Mmmmmm, mmmm, Oh God," as a warm stickiness spilled across Brandon's stomach.

"Fuck! Aww, fuck," Noah gasped out.

"Move."

"What?"

"Move now."

Noah quickly slid off Brandon just as Brandon's world exploded and came back together again. His semen mixed with Noah's on his belly.

Noah collapsed onto Brandon, kissing him violently, smearing the mess between them

"Shit, Noah. We made a nice mess."

Noah just snickered and lowered his head against Brandon's bare shoulder. "Thank you." He brushed his cheek against Brandon's shoulder. Brandon put his arm around him protectively.

"No need to thank me, Noah." Brandon turned his head and kissed Noah's forehead several times. "Who am I to deny the man I care so much for if he wants to make love to me?"

Noah let out a sigh.

Brandon thought about his father's old watch. Perhaps that would make a good present for Noah. That pocket watch had been in the family for a long time. He thought he would enjoy the idea of Noah having the watch.

"Noah, I'm going to run to the bunkhouse. I have something I would like you to have."

Noah sat up. "Don't be gone too long."

"I won't." Brandon stood up and began getting dressed. He looked back at Noah, stretched out on a hay bale. God, what a beautiful sight! Brandon tried hard to photograph that moment mentally. Maybe now Noah would understand. He wasn't so broken he couldn't be loved. Humming a happy tune, Brandon left the barn.

Chapter Five

Noah watched Brandon leave the barn. God... Could this work out for them? Was he truly not too broken to have a relationship? If that were so, what did he have with Mason and Ian? Close friends he slept with occasionally? No. He *was* broken. No one could ever truly and deeply love him for who he was... Except maybe Brandon.

Noah reached over and grabbed his clothes. The only sounds were the cows shifting their feet and the occasional moo.

What could Brandon be getting? He ran out of there like a bat out of hell.

Noah was fastening his jeans when a sinister laugh echoed through the air, breaking the peace.

"So, you really are a sissy boy."

Noah quickly stood up and faced his biological father.

"How many dicks do you take up your ass, sissy boy? Just his or every guy on this damned farm?" Mark's face twisted into a mask of humor and disgust.

"Get the hell away from me." Noah backed away a couple of steps.

"Or you'll what, sissy boy? Slap me?" Mark chuckled.

"There's a restraining order, and you shouldn't even be here. I could easily..."

"You think a piece of paper is going to stop me? I'm your father. And besides, it's not in effect anymore, and maybe now I can go back to making my boy a man."

"If you lay a hand on me, the others will ask questions."

"Who's going to tell, Noah? You?" Mark stepped closer, almost in arm's reach.

Noah backed right up to the door of the cow's pen. He had nowhere else to go. He was trapped between Mark and the pen. Maybe he could go left or right and dodge any move Mark made.

"Now, tell dad how many dicks you've been taking up your ass like the sissy boy you are."

"I said get the hell away from me, you sick fuck, or I'll scream."

Mark jumped forward just as Noah was about to open his mouth. "You let out a sound, and I'll pummel you within an inch of your life." He took a step back after Noah closed his mouth.

"There, now listen to me and listen good. You tell them who I am, and you will regret it. Do you understand me? This job is the first piece of luck I've had since I got out of jail, and I'll be damned if a sissy boy like you is going to ruin it for me."

"You brought all this shit on yourself. I had nothing to do with it."

"Bullshit. Who went running to the neighbor? Who called the cops? It had to be you. Do I make myself clear? Do you understand what I'm telling you?" Mark made a fist.

Noah braced himself for a hit. He watched as Mark's fist came down quickly. He closed his eyes, but nothing happened. He opened them to see Mark snickering.

"Still flinching like a fucking baby. Will you ever stop being a fucking disgrace to me, boy?"

"You're sick!"

"Me?" Mark's eyebrows shot up. "I'm the sick one? I'm not the one getting fucked in the ass every night, sissy boy." Mark took a step forward.

"I said get the hell away from me." Noah moved right like he was going to make a run for it. When Mark stepped right to block him, Noah took his chance and made a mad dash to the left. He only managed to get a few steps before he felt Mark's hand take hold of the back of his shirt and pull him back into place.

Noah struggled, but Mark was still stronger than him. Mark pushed Noah against the pen door again so hard that Noah's head exploded, and his vision was filled with stars. "The fuck!"

"Looks like I'm going to have to beat the sissy out of you, boy! I'll teach you to disgrace the Easton name."

"No, please don't hurt me."

Mark sighed. "I'll make you a deal. Leave now, and I won't hurt anyone else." He pulled a lighter out of his pocket, flipped the top, and started to light it.

"Leave?"

"This place isn't big enough for both of us. You leave, and I won't set fire to the house."

"You wouldn't."

"Rob you of your newfound family? Why not?"

"Mark, please, I..."

"Maybe if you leave now, I won't do it with everyone still inside."

Noah tried to pull free from Mark, but Mark's grip was like iron. He couldn't get free, struggle as he might.

Mark brought the lighter down close to Noah's shirt. "Maybe I'll start with you."

Noah closed his eyes and waited, but nothing happened. When Noah opened his eyes, Mark had put out the lighter and dropped it back in his pocket. "Nah, that would be too easy." He sighed. "I guess it's my fist, then." He raised his fist, ready to clock Noah.

The adrenaline running through him was beating in time with Noah's heartbeat. He wasn't going to be able to escape. He struggled hard to pull away, but Mark held him fast.

"Stop moving, and it will go a lot easier."

"Fuck you, you bastard."

"Ohhh, now you wanna fuck your father? Does your path of depravity ever end?"

The thought turned Noah's stomach. He had to find a way out, some way to escape.

"Are you ready for your beating, sissy boy?"

Unable to move, Noah could only wait for the inevitable. He saw Mark lift his fist, ready to strike.

Noah closed his eyes. It was nothing new. The sooner it was over, the better off he would be.

Suddenly there was a loud noise to the left.

"Noah!" a voice cried out.

Almost instantly, Noah felt pulled and staggered, but then he was free. He moved quickly back to his place and looked to see what was going on.

Brandon was straddling Mark, sending fist after fist into his gut. Noah quickly looked around for anything that would help. He looked back at Brandon and Mark.

Mark had gained the upper hand and was on top, sending a fist at Brandon's head, howling, "How dare you do that to him, you sick bastard. I saw what you guys were doing earlier. Are you so hard up for sex?"

Noah quickly started looking around. There had to be a weapon or something. He couldn't let Mark do this to Brandon.

Something. Anything. Nothing!

Brandon and Mark rolled again; this time, Brandon managed to get free. He moved to block Mark from getting to Noah.

"What the hell is going on here? What were you going to do to Noah?"

"It's none of your business."

Brandon made fists and stepped up to swing, but Noah quickly moved from behind Brandon and put a hand on his chest. "No, please don't."

"Noah, what the hell are you doing?"

"I can't let you do this."

Brandon's eyes widened as he asked, "Why not?"

Noah closed his eyes. This nightmare was getting worse and worse. He opened his eyes, looking into the anger in Brandon's eyes. "Because Mark is my father." After a moment, Noah repeated his words. "Mark is my biological father."

The look of shock on Brandon's face was quickly replaced by even more rage. He took a step to go after Mark again, but Noah used his entire body to block Brandon from moving.

"You can't do this. Trust me. He's not worth it."

"Come on, hot shot. Come pop me one again," Mark sneered, wiping blood from his nose.

"It's not worth it," Noah pleaded. He had to get this through Brandon's head somehow, but how?

A look of disbelief replaced Brandon's rage. "What the hell, Noah?" Brandon glared at Mark.

Noah noticed a bruise was forming on Brandon's face. That would be very hard to explain without going into too much detail.

"Are you telling me this is the bastard who used to beat you while you were growing up? Is that what you're telling me, Noah?"

"Yes."

The hatred and anger in Brandon's eyes sent a chill down Noah's spine, and he was thankful that rage was not turned on him.

Mark pulled his lighter out of his pocket and opened the lid, starting the flame. "Remember what I said, Noah." And he tossed the lit lighter on the pile of hay before turning to leave the barn.

The hay caught in a moment, and Brandon quickly moved for the fire extinguisher hanging on the wall. With a few short bursts, the fire was out. Brandon took a deep breath and then turned to Noah. "Are you okay?"

"Yes, I'm fine, just a little shaken up." Noah stepped up to Brandon, who put his arms around him.

The minute Noah felt Brandon's protective arms, all his emotions exploded, and he began to cry. All the emotions came out with his tears.

"Hey, shhh, Noah, it will be okay. I got you. I got you. I'm not going to let anything happen to you."

Like anyone could protect him except himself. Noah pulled away from Brandon and wiped his tears.

"You need to tell Mason what happened."

"I can't." Noah turned away from Brandon.

"Why not?" Brandon carefully braced Noah's shoulders and gently turned him to face him. The bruise on his face was starting to change color and become apparent.

"Mark has threatened to hurt everyone if I don't leave."

"What can he do?"

"Brandon," Noah began, "my father is crazy. He was seriously out of his mind. He's so messed up from all the drugs and alcohol, it screwed up his head. He's seriously sick, and I'm inclined to believe any threat he makes."

"Don't try to defend that asshole to me. There is no excuse for the way he treated you."

"Brandon, please, I have to go. I can't stay here with him. I have to go."

"All the more reason to..."

Noah put his hand on Brandon's chest, and Brandon took it carefully, kissing the tips of his fingers.

"No, I can't tell Mason. Mark threatened to harm everyone. You don't know what all that man is capable of like I do. Please, Brandon, if you care about me as much as you say you do, please take me away from here."

"Will that honestly make you feel safe?" Brandon waited patiently for an answer.

Was anywhere really and truly safe from Mark? Even though he'd thought he was safe, Mark had still managed to find him. Would he be able to find him if he went anywhere else?

"Please?" Noah pleaded.

Brandon sighed heavily. "I still think you're making a big mistake." He put his arms around Noah calmly. "But your safety needs to come first. I promise to take you away from here only on the condition that at some point, you'll tell Mason what happened and who Mark is."

Noah sighed with relief. "Then let's go now, please."

"Come with me. Could you wait for me in my truck? Lock the doors and don't come out. I'll be back as soon as I gather a few things. Do you have clothes that you can go get?"

"I don't wanna go back to the house. What if Mark's there?"

"Do you think he would try anything with Mason and Mrs. Dale there? Go get your stuff and meet me at my truck."

"I'd rather stay locked in the truck."

Brandon sighed.

Come on, see that that is the best course of action, Noah thought. He knew Mark had to be either at the house or the bunkhouse. He didn't feel like having another round with the man. "Please just let me stay here. Get your stuff, and I'll wait here. I promise."

Brandon escorted Noah to the truck and opened the passenger door. "Lock the doors and stay put. I'll be only a few moments."

Noah climbed into the truck's cab, locked his door, and then leaned over and locked the driver's door. Brandon disappeared towards the bunkhouse. After a little while, he returned with a small plastic grocery sack and unlocked the door. Soon, he was inside, and the two took off, leaving Dale Farm far behind.

Chapter Six

Brandon took a deep breath and then flipped on the windshield wipers on his truck.

They had left Dale Farm twenty minutes ago, and the rain had started coming down shortly after that. It wasn't a hard rain, but it made driving difficult. Another five minutes to go before they entered Remington City.

As they approached the next intersection, Brandon brought the truck to a stop and glanced at Noah.

Noah's head lay against the doorframe, his eyes were closed, and his chest raised and lowered gently. He had a good-size bruise forming on his arm, which Brandon assumed was a parting gift from Mark.

And that was another thing. Why didn't Noah want Mason to know he'd accidentally hired the bastard? Why suffer in silence? What kind of hold did Mark have over Noah, besides being his biological father?

Brandon took off again, and a green sign with reflective tape alerted him that Remington City was five miles away. At this trajectory, when they reached the outskirts of town, there was a truck stop/gas station they could stop at for a break. But then what? Where would they go? What would they do for food and shelter?

Brandon pulled the truck into the gas station portion of the truck stop at one of the pumps. Next to him, Noah began to stir. His eyes fluttered open, and he sat upright, trying to stretch against the seat belt holding him in place. "Where are we?" He tried to stifle a yawn.

Brandon pointed to the gas station sign. "We're at a gas station on the outskirts of Remington City." After a moment, he continued. "Why don't you go in and get cleaned up? I need to fill the tank. They may have T-shirts in there. You can buy one and change."

Noah nodded.

The awning over the front of the store provided Noah sufficient cover as he climbed out of the truck and headed inside the store.

No sooner than Brandon had moved the truck to the pump, Noah came running back outside, shamefully climbing back in the truck.

"You okay?"

"Too many people in there. I can't do it."

Brandon sighed with disappointment and sadness. Both because he wished for Noah's sake he could face his fears. He gassed up the truck and popped back into the truck's cabin for his wallet. "You want anything from inside?"

Noah shook his head. "No, thank you."

"I'll go in with you. You'll need fresh clothes since you didn't get your stuff before we left."

"It was impossible." Noah shot Brandon a wan smile. "It's not like I haven't worn the same clothes for days before."

"Don't look at me like that. I lived on the streets for four years. I didn't always have access to fresh clothing."

"Well, if we don't figure out something, you will be again. Do you have any ideas?"

Noah shook his head again. "Not really. I have about eighteen dollars cash from my last allowance."

Brandon opened his wallet and started counting bills. He had enough to pay for gas and maybe a night at a motel, but that was it. "I could probably cover us one night somewhere."

Noah readjusted in his seat and fastened his seat belt. "At least that's something. He turned to Brandon. "I mean, if push comes to shove, we could sleep in the truck or go to one of the shelters. There are three of them in Remington City. Most of them know me well by now."

Brandon didn't like the idea of staying at a shelter. He had heard horror stories about many of them, but if Noah was okay with it... Oh, but was he? Noah's eyes looked bloodshot, and he looked like what he needed was a hot meal and a good night's sleep. Brandon felt the same way. "Are you hungry?"

"No, thanks anyway. I don't think I could eat if I tried."

Brandon climbed out of the truck and paid for the gas before returning to Noah. He moved the truck from the pump and re-parked in a spot far from the front door before killing the engine. Outside, the rain had started coming down in droves again. It sounded almost peaceful against the metal of the truck.

This was all starting to be too much. Brandon rested his elbows on the steering wheel and hid his face in his hands. He raised his head and turned to look at Noah.

"What just happened?"

Noah sat in silence and looked out the window.

"Noah, talk to me, please."

Noah turned to look at Brandon. "It's an old story. I've told you a bit of it already."

"I seem to have plenty of time." Brandon crossed his arms over his chest.

Noah bit his lip and looked away.

"Noah, please? I may have just sacrificed my job and livelihood for you. I want an answer."

"Mark Easton—or Jennings, as he calls himself now—is the reason I'm all screwed up." Noah's bottom lip began to quiver.

Shit! Was this a bad idea? Maybe he should stop Noah from continuing, but he continued his story before Brandon had the chance.

"When I was growing up, my father took his anger, frustrations, and drug withdrawal out on me. A couple of times my moth—Kelly tried to intercede, but he would beat her senselessly. Eventually, she gave up, and I hate her for it."

"Oh my God, Noah." Brandon's heart fell into his stomach. The thought of anyone touching Noah in anger or cruelty was starting to make his temper roll. "You don't have to tell me any more if you—"

Noah held up a hand. "But I do. I want to. I want you to know what you're getting into with me."

Brandon was hesitant but nodded for Noah to continue.

"The cops and social workers came to our house regularly, but Mark is a clever man. He would always manage to convince them that nothing was wrong. Eventually, Kelly would help. She had every opportunity to get us the hell out of there, and she failed to do so, another reason I hate her."

"Kelly's your mother?"

"Yes."

"She's the lady who came to the farm this morning?"

"Yes."

A crack of thunder filled the cabin, and Noah jumped. After a short moment of calming breaths, he continued, "On the day of my eighteenth birthday, my father got drunk and started beating me. I managed to escape to a park and stayed there all night."

"Noah, if this is too painful..."

Noah held up his hand again. "Let me finish."

"Okay."

"I returned to the house, but the police were there. I overheard one cop tell the other what had happened and why my father was now in the back of a squad car. I never saw him or Kelly again after that." Noah took a deep breath. "After that, I spent the next four years on the streets struggling to stay alive. Then one day, I tried pickpocketing the right person, Daddy James. He took pity on me and took me home with him, and the rest, as they say, is history."

Brandon soaked in Noah's words before he spoke. "This man is dangerous. All the more reason for you to tell Mason what's going on, Noah."

Noah started crying at that point. "Don't you think I would if I could?"

"Why can't you?"

"Because."

"Because why?"

"Just because, that's why."

Irritation filled Brandon, and he slammed his fists into the steering wheel. "Dammit, Noah, now is not the time to play games here."

"Fine!" Noah growled. "He threatened to set fire to the house with everyone inside if I told them who he was. He's crazy, Brandon. I told you that."

"He threatened you?"

"Knowing him, it's not an idle threat. He would do it. Hurt Daddy Mason, Ian, Grammy. They've all meant a lot to me, and I couldn't bear it if one of them got hurt. He would do it to spite me." Noah let out a fresh set of sobs before he tried to regain his self-composure. He was failing miserably.

Brandon ached to reach out and put his arm around him, but his irritation and anger were holding him in place.

"As long as I'm gone, they will be safe, okay? Are you fucking happy now?"

"No, Noah, I'm not happy." Brandon took a deep breath. He needed to control his temper, or he would not be any use to himself, let alone Noah.

When Brandon looked up, Noah was cringing at the far end of the truck cabin, a wild look of terror on his face.

Dammit. Brandon closed his eyes and counted to five and then five again. He opened them to see Noah's wide eyes, eyebrows scrunched.

"Noah... Oh, Noah, I'm sorry for losing my temper." Brandon tried to offer Noah a half smile, but that felt fake, and he wasn't at all sure that Noah would accept his apology. He tried reaching out to Noah and held his hand between them. Noah just glanced at Brandon's hand and then back at Brandon as if to say, *What do you want me to do with that? Are you going to use it?*

Brandon pulled his hand back. Fuck, what the hell had he just done? Noah's father had done a number on him. Then

Brandon had let his temper scare the hell out of Noah. Had Brandon expected any different response? How could he be sure Noah could have a happy, healthy relationship? Honestly, he wasn't sure how Mason and Ian still played in this arrangement.

"Noah, you say you care about everyone at Dale Farm and are trying to protect them, correct?"

"I don't wanna talk about this anymore."

"Just hear me out."

Hesitantly, Noah turned to face Brandon. "Okay."

"If your father is such a psychopath, don't you think he might do something even if you aren't there?"

"I don't think so. It's always been me he liked to torment the most—me or Kelly, and she's long gone. I doubt he will try anything as long as I stay away."

Brandon sighed. Noah was going for martyrdom, and his mind was made up. So the best course of action for Brandon was to ride this ride with him as far as it went.

Everyone at Dale Farm should have realized by now that they were both missing. Should he call and at least tell Mason that they were okay?

Noah's voice cut through his thoughts. "I think I know where we can stay. Can I borrow your phone?"

Brandon dug his phone out of his pocket and handed it over. Noah pulled a small business card out of his wallet and dialed the number.

After a brief conversation with the person on the other end, Noah hung up and handed the phone back. "We need to go now."

"Just direct me."

Brandon started the truck, and the two went farther into the city.

Chapter Seven

Caleb Olivera sat quietly in the comfort of his condo. He had just gotten off the phone and kicked off his shoes. It had been a long day at the office. He took a deep breath and closed his eyes. Everything hurt. He should try to find a new office chair. The one he had was starting to kill his back, being in it all day. After the weekend, he would have to talk with his office assistant to place the order.

"Daddy Caleb?" A strawberry-blond young man with short hair and a beard entered the living room. He was slim with an oval face. His lower body was covered in paint on tight blue jeans. His shirtless top was covered only by a leather harness.

"Oh, shit, Luke, I'm sorry. We're about to have company."

Luke's face fell. "Who?"

"Noah and that farmhand of Mason's." When Noah had first called, Caleb had forgotten he had given Noah his business card the night they spent in the hospital waiting to hear word on Mrs. Dale, after her heart attack. What a wonderful woman she was. So warm and caring. A bit of a spitfire, which Caleb could appreciate. She had to be to raise a wonderful gentleman like Mason.

Caleb smiled at the thought of his primary. It was hard to believe that it had already been five months since the boys set them up on that first blind date. How time flew! Even though for a moment there, he'd thought he had fucked everything up. Just as long as Mason never found out that Caleb himself made the payment that saved the farm from his blunder.

"Daddy Caleb? Anyone home?" Luke waved his hand in front of Caleb's face.

Caleb caught Luke's hand and kissed the back of it. "Sorry boy, what?"

"I said, why are Noah and the farmhand coming here?"

"I don't know. Noah said he needed to talk to me." Caleb hoped nothing was wrong with Mason or his mother.

Almost as if on cue, the doorbell rang.

Luke moved to answer it. "Noah, good to see you, buddy."

"Luke, you remember Brandon?"

"Of course. Come on in, both of you."

A blond-haired short man followed a taller man with brown hair and a dancer's frame. Both kept their focus on Luke, not their surroundings, so Caleb had a chance to study them. The man he remembers as Noah looked nervous, while the other man watched him with worry in his eyes.

"We're here to see Caleb. Is he around? He said he would be."

"Yes, just through there." Luke pointed towards the living room.

"Good to see you, Noah." Caleb stood up as Noah and Brandon entered. "Who's your friend?"

Noah offered his hand. Caleb took it, shook it, and turned to Brandon.

"Brandon Carsey, I would like you to meet Caleb Olivera. I believe you may have met briefly when we were at the hospital. Brandon is a farmhand out at Dale Farm."

Caleb extended a hand to Brandon, who took it with an excellent grip. Caleb liked that.

"Very briefly."

"Now, let's all sit down, and you can tell me what's up." Caleb motioned for both young men to have a seat across from him on the sectional.

As soon as everyone was seated, Noah cleared his throat and started. "I need a big favor."

Caleb turned his hand palm up. "Okay."

Noah glanced at Brandon, who nodded gently before Noah continued. "We need a place to stay for a couple of days."

"Whoa, what?"

"We wanted to know if we could stay with you for a few days."

"Noah, does Mason know you're here?"

"No, Mason doesn't know we're here."

"Why not?"

"It's difficult to explain." Noah's eyes locked on the ground. Caleb couldn't tell if he was being bashful or what was happening with him. From what Mason had told him, Noah had had a rough life, but he didn't go into too much detail. *What had he said?* He'd first met Noah after Noah tried to pickpocket his late husband?

"You know, I'm going to need something more to go on before I can say yes."

Caleb's mind was a whirl. Did something happen between him and Mason? Should he call Mason and get his side of the story first? Was Mason going to be unhappy if Caleb let Noah stay here?

A headache was barely starting to form, and Caleb realized the only way to find out was to ask. "Did something happen at the farm?"

"Yes, but I can't tell you. I can't let it get back to Daddy Mason. Please, can Brandon and I stay here?"

"Noah, listen. You know damn well that Mason and I are seeing each other. You're going to run into him eventually."

"I hope so. Because I do care a great deal for Daddy Mason and Ian, but things are complicated at Dale Farm right now."

"They can't be that bad." Caleb regretted saying it the moment it left his lips. Brandon was looking away, his eyes closed, lip curled up in a wince.

Maybe it *was* that bad. "Mason is probably worried sick about you. You need to tell him you're here."

Noah let out a sigh, and his shoulders went down. He stood, though Brandon stayed seated.

"It's okay. We'll figure something else out."

Shit! Caleb, you numskull! If he's here, he'll be safe, and Mason will know where he is staying. Whatever the problem was at Dale Farm, securing Noah was the most important thing he needed to worry about at this time.

Brandon stood up. "Thanks anyway, Mr. Olivera."

"Wait, Noah." Caleb reached out and took hold of his arm. "I didn't say you couldn't stay. Luke, please prepare the guest room for Noah and Brandon."

Luke stood and headed for the stairs with a nod and a half smile.

"I'm confused." Noah pulled his arm gently out of Caleb's grasp.

"I'd rather you stayed here." Caleb pointed at the stairs. "Besides, Mason will know you're safe if you're here. I want to make it clear. I will tell him you're here and will be my guest for a few days. Anything else is your business. Do we have a deal?"

"Fine. I guess I'll have to live with it." Noah's shoulders slumped.

Brandon piped up just then. "At least this way, we won't be sleeping in my truck."

Noah nodded in agreement.

"Noah," Caleb began, "can you give me an idea of how long you plan to stay?"

"I don't know. It depends on how long it takes to resolve things at Daddy Mason's place."

"I see. Well..." Caleb slapped his thighs and stood up. "Luke should have your room ready by now. It's the last door on the right up the stairs here."

"Thank you." Noah and Brandon headed up the stairs together.

Those two seemed glued at the hip. Caleb snickered. *Good for you, boy. I hope it works out.*

Now, where was his cell phone? He needed to call Mason and let him know that Noah and Brandon were here and safe.

Caleb located his phone, scanned for Mason's number, and hit send.

After two rings, a voice answered. "Hello?"

"Hello, can I speak with Mason please?"

"Who's calling?"

"Caleb."

"Oh, my knight in shining armor."

"How are you, Mrs. Dale?"

"No, Carrie, please, and I'm fine. Mason is out at the barn. He... Wait a minute."

Caleb heard some mumbled conversation before Mason's deep rich voice answered. "Hello?"

"Hi, sexy."

"Hey yourself."

"You missing anyone?"

"Noah and Brandon. Are they with you?"

"Yes. They're here, and they're safe."

"Damn. I'm on my way."

"Mason, hold up."

"What?"

"Noah's a wreck. The boy and your farmhand just crashed for the night. It's rather late. It would probably be better to come in the morning."

"Those two have some explaining to do. I found a bunch of hay burned in the barn, and they're nowhere to be found. If either of them were responsible..." Mason trailed off.

"Mason, Noah is scared to death. Said things were difficult at the farm right now. Do you have any idea what he's talking about at all? He hasn't told me anything."

"Not a clue. I'm just as dumbfounded as you are, to be honest."

"Okay, let's let cooler heads prevail. Come tomorrow."

"Bright and early."

"Agreed."

"Good night, my sexy man." And Mason hung up.

Caleb clicked his phone off and headed for bed. Hopefully, talking to Mason was the right thing to do. At least he now knew where Noah was, but what was this burned hay business? Had they accidentally started a fire? Noah and Brandon didn't seem like the type to have done something like that without saying something to someone.

Caleb yawned as he prepared for bed.

And what about Noah? The boy was traumatized. Anyone who knew him could see it in his mannerisms, and others noticed. Caleb didn't know how to proceed. Probably the best thing to do was let Mason handle it when he got here in the morning. Less chance of getting in trouble that way.

Caleb put his clothes in his laundry delivery bag and climbed into bed. He was asleep before his head hit the pillow.

Chapter Eight

Noah's eyes fluttered open, and he was greeted by morning light flooding the room.

It took him only a moment to remember he was not at Dale Farm. He tried to move, but Brandon's arm lay over his waist and hip. How warm and soft Brandon felt pressed up against him.

But his bladder was screaming for release. He carefully dislodged himself and slid out of bed. The full-size bed must have been the same one Grammy Carrie had stayed in during her recovery.

If Caleb went through with his phone call to Daddy Mason, Noah would have to face him at some point today. What was he going to tell him?

Oh, yeah, you hired the bastard who beat me and destroyed my life, maybe?

Noah had to protect them, and if that meant staying far away from Dale Farm, then so be it.

He flipped on the bathroom light, used the bathroom, and caught a glimpse of himself in the mirror. A horrible blue mark graced his left forearm from where Mark had grabbed him.

Noah glanced into his eyes in the mirror. They had bags and were still red from crying the night before.

Last night, after they had retired for the night, Brandon had been so sweet. He had spooned Noah, telling him it would be alright and they would work things out.

But would it be alright? Daddy Mason would be here at some point today, and Noah dreaded it. He didn't know if he could face the man who had done so much for him.

Telling Daddy Mason about Mark was utterly out of the question, but would he be able to protect him by lying? Noah had never been any good at it. Mason would see right through him. Omitting the truth was one thing, but outright lying?

Noah turned on the cold water tap and splashed some on his face. He would have to ask Drake, Luke's pup, if he had an extra outfit or two he could wear since he couldn't get any of his clothes before he left. The two were almost the same build and size, so Drake might have something he could borrow.

Maybe he could call Ian and ask him to bring him some of his clothes from the farm. No, because his adopted big brother would ask a thousand questions, and dealing with Daddy Mason was going to be bad enough.

Noah dried his face and returned to his and Brandon's room.

Brandon was still asleep. His naked chest rose and fell in gentle waves.

A wistful smile tugged at the corner of Noah's mouth. Brandon had been so good to him. Thank God he showed up when he did. Had he not shown up, Mark would have beaten Noah again. Trying to explain to the others about the bruises would be rough.

Noah slid back into bed and glanced out the nearby curtain. The city was already alive and jumping outside. He turned to Brandon and kissed his forehead.

Brandon was one of the good ones.

If Noah wasn't so broken, he could easily fall in love with the man. But there was too much internal damage... Or was there?

Brandon's eyes blinked open, and then he squeezed them shut, covering them with his hand. "Aww fuck."

"Good morning."

"Morning."

"Sleep well?"

"Not really."

"I'm sorry."

Brandon struggled to sit up. He stared out, blinked his eyes a couple of times, and then, without a second thought, fell back on the pillows again.

Noah giggled. "Not a morning person, I take it?"

"Not really."

Noah rubbed the top of Brandon's head gently. "You poor man. How did you survive working at Dale Farm when everyone gets up at sunrise?"

"By the skin of my teeth and lots and lots of coffee."

Noah smiled.

A knock at the door sounded "Hey guys, breakfast is ready," Luke proclaimed in his most dramatic voice.

Noah and Brandon locked eyes, and both broke out in laughter. Noah climbed out of bed and quickly turned to Brandon. "I hope for your sake they have coffee. I can't stand the stuff."

Brandon threw off the covers and slowly pulled on his clothes. Once he was dressed, the two headed off for the kitchen.

"Good morning, sleepyheads." Luke flipped a pancake from the skillet he was standing over.

"Good morning." Noah took a seat at the table.

"Coffee?" Brandon asked.

"Over at the coffeemaker. Help yourself to what's on the table."

Brandon went to fetch himself a cup.

"I've got pancakes and sausages for breakfast. I hope that will be okay."

"Sounds good to me." Brandon took a sip of his coffee and sat next to Noah.

"Where are Caleb and Drake?" Noah helped himself to a stack of flapjacks.

"Daddy Caleb is with Mason in the other room. Daddy Mason came early this morning, and Drake left for work already."

Noah's heart fell into his stomach. Daddy Mason was here? Shit! He was going to be so angry. So hurt. *I don't want to face him.* On the other hand, Noah at least owed him that much after everything.

"Good morning, everyone." The sound of Daddy Mason's voice sent sweet agony through Noah. He took a deep breath and turned to face him.

"Good morning, Noah." Caleb motioned for Luke and Brandon to leave the room with him so the two could talk.

Noah wanted to cry out for them to please don't leave him.

Brandon was the last to leave. He issued Noah a half smile before disappearing through the archway.

Noah was alone with Mason. Noah stood as his daddy bear came into the room.

"Please have a seat, Noah. We need to talk."

Noah took a seat, held his breath, expecting the worse as Mason sat near him.

Mason ran a hand through his brown hair and looked away for a moment. He then turned to Noah, care and confusion coming from his gentle brown eyes. "Noah, my boy, what's going on?"

You can't tell him, Noah, a voice in his head called out. *You must protect him and everyone at Dale Farm for his own sake.*

Noah shook his head. "I just can't come back to the farm."

"Why not? Did something happen that I'm not aware of, kiddo? Did Brandon do something he shouldn't have?"

"No, nothing like that. Brandon's been beyond amazing. It's just that..." Come on, Noah, think of something quickly. "I've been giving it a lot of thought, and I don't think it's working anymore."

Daddy Mason did a double take. "What?" After a short pause, he continued. "This is coming out of the left field." Mason took a deep breath. "If it's about the fire in the barn, it didn't do any damage. What happened, anyway?"

Noah bit his lip. He should have hidden the charred hay. What had he been thinking?

"That was an accident," Noah stated, looking away from Mason. Damn, he hated lying. Mason would see right through him if he wasn't careful.

"And Brandon? Does he still want his job?"

"I don't know. You'll have to ask him."

Mason rested his face in his hands and let out a slightly frustrated growl. He lowered his hands, staring right at Noah. "Boy, I know something is wrong. Why won't you tell me?"

"I can't. That's all, Daddy Mason. I want to stay here. Brandon and I will try to get a place, and then we'll see from there."

"Was it me? Did I do something?"

"No, Mason, you didn't do anything. I promise it wasn't you. It wasn't Ian or Grammy Carrie. I promise."

"Then what?"

"I can't tell you. I'm sorry."

"This isn't right, boy. Please, kiddo. Tell Daddy what's wrong. What happened to make you just up and leave like this?"

"I'm sorry, Daddy Mason. I love you and Ian, and Grammy, and God knows I loved James, but..." Noah could feel his emotions stinging his eyes. The waterworks would start if he didn't get through this and get through it quickly. All he needed was for Mason to see him crying.

Mason's face fell with the mention of his late husband. James had been the catalyst that brought Noah into this family.

"There's no need for you to be sorry. Just tell me what's going on so I can make it right."

"Nothing is wrong." God, Noah hated lying, but he had to protect the family that had done so much for him. He didn't know what he would do to convince this man, who knew Noah better than anyone else.

"Please talk to me, Noah."

"I have been talking to you. Please don't make this harder than it needs to be."

"It doesn't need to be hard. You just have to talk to me, kiddo."

Noah wished he could make Mason understand that he was trying to protect him and everyone. They had no idea what Mark was capable of when he was pushed.

Tears started to spill from Noah's eyes, and he wiped them away and sniffled. He stood up, ready to flee, when Mason stood up and tried to put his arms around him.

Noah just backed off. God, this was killing him. The look on Mason's face turned Noah's blood to ice.

"I'm sorry, Dadd—I mean Mason. But I can't come back, and I can't tell you why."

Mason's face fell, defeated. "Well, kiddo, if that's what you truly want..."

It wasn't what Noah wanted, but he didn't have much choice. He couldn't return while Mark was there, or the harassment would continue. Noah couldn't tell, or Mark would hurt or kill someone Noah truly loved and cared about with all his heart. It was a matter of being cruel to be kind.

"I guess there isn't anything more to say." Mason's face was a mask of sorrow. Noah's whole being ached to put his arms around his daddy bear and comfort him. Tell him it was all a lie and that he would return today to Dale Farm. A place he had thought of as his own Neverland. A place he never had to grow up.

"I guess not."

Mason turned to the arch and headed out. Before he passed through, he turned back for a moment. "I will never stop loving you, boy, and I will always be your daddy. I don't understand this, whatever it is going on, but if and when you are ready to return, you will always have a home with me on the farm."

Tears started streaming down Noah's face. Why did Mason have to be such a good man? God, this was killing him.

"Goodbye, Noah. Daddy loves you and always will."

Choked up on his emotions, Noah only nodded.

Mason looked towards his feet for a moment with despair and then made his exit.

Once he was out of sight, Noah collapsed into a chair, head down on the table, and began to cry.

Chapter Nine

Brandon looked up as Mason entered the living room. Never in all the time had he known the middle-aged farmer had he seen Mason so hurt and crestfallen.

Mason glanced around the room. Caleb stood and moved to put an arm around Mason, but he shrugged it off.

Luke then stood, but Caleb held up a hand. "No."

Luke sighed and sat back down.

What had Noah said to upset Mason? Did Noah tell him about Mark?

"I just don't know what is going on with that boy. Did I do something wrong?" Mason covered his eyes with his hand.

It was killing Brandon to see Mason so upset. The man had been shaken to his core. Did Noah mean so much to him? What did that mean for Brandon and Noah?

Luke retook his seat.

God, this situation was getting worse.

"No, Mason," Brandon finally said. "You didn't do anything wrong."

Mason turned to him. His eyes were red. "Do you know what's going on? Why did you and Noah leave?"

Shit! Should he open his mouth and say something? Noah was not very happy here. He was happier at Dale Farm. What had Noah said?

"I do, but it's not my place to say. I'm sorry."

Mason slapped the side of his massive thighs. "I guess there's nothing more to be done." After a moment or two, Mason asked, "Are you returning to work or..."

"I'm going to stay here with Noah. I know I'm leaving you in the lurch, but I'm very concerned about him and want to ensure he'll be okay."

Mason let out a heavy sigh. "Okay." He turned, put his arms around Caleb, and kissed him. Then without another word, Mason headed out the door.

Caleb was hot on his heels. "Man, I'll walk you out."

"That won't be—"

Caleb cut him off. "I insist."

That was all it took. Mason shrugged and was out the door, Caleb following close behind.

Brandon turned to head into the kitchen. He needed to talk to Noah.

Noah sat with his head on the table. His back rose and fell as he sobbed.

Brandon's heart jumped to his throat. He hated seeing Noah cry.

Unable to come up with words, Brandon sat next to Noah and placed his hand on Noah's back.

Noah shot up quickly the minute he was touched and tried to dry his red eyes.

"Shit." Noah looked away from Brandon.

"I'm sorry. I didn't mean to startle you. Are you okay?"

Noah stared back. His eyes asked if Brandon had lost his mind. "What do you think? I just broke the heart of one of the rare few men in my life who was ever good to me."

"You didn't have to, Noah."

"God, Brandon. What is it going to take to get you to understand?"

"Look, I know you're not happy with this situation. Why are you letting him do this to you?"

"Because I don't have a choice, that's why."

Brandon scooted back in his chair. "Don't have a choice? You always have a choice. And you chose to bail."

Noah's shocked, hurt look sent a surge of triumph through Brandon. He stood to leave the room.

The truth hurt sometimes, and right now, Noah needed to hear the truth.

Before Brandon could reach the door, Noah's hand shot out and grabbed his arm. "How dare you?"

"How dare I? Easily. It would help if you had the truth, not some mixed-up notion you have going on in your head. Your father is nothing more than a bully, and he has control of you."

Noah let go of Brandon. "You don't know what you're talking about, so please leave it alone. My father is dangerous. You don't know what he is capable of doing. Please don't get angry. Trust me that I'm doing the right thing. I know what I'm doing."

"What you're doing is wrong on so many levels." Brandon fought to find the words to convey the anger and disappointment, but any thoughts that came wouldn't do any good. If he let his anger rage, Noah would be terrified of him, and where would he be? "You know what? I don't want to fight about this anymore. You do you, Noah. You know you have my support, but I still think you are making a mistake. I'm going to walk away before I say something we both regret."

As he turned to leave, Brandon came face-to-face with Luke.

"Whoa, man, where's the fire?"

Brandon muttered an "excuse me" and sidestepped Luke without reply. He had to get away from Noah for a moment or two to breathe.

Maybe a drive would clear his head. After grabbing his keys, Brandon headed out to his truck.

The questions began as soon as Brandon was in his truck and driving.

God, had he done the right thing?

He pretty much walked away from his job at Dale Farm for Noah. He had to protect him, but had he done the right thing? Only time would tell.

How could he get it through Noah's thick head that all of this was fixable and all he had to do was open his damned mouth and tell someone? If Mason knew the whole story, Mark would be history.

His father's voice seeped into his head. *You can lead a horse to water, but you can't make him drink.* Oh, how that old saying was true!

Brandon flipped on the radio, flooding the car with a sweet country love song. After a few minutes, the song started grating on his nerves, and he switched it off. All it did was make him think of Noah. That beautiful boy, inside and out, needed someone to help him but didn't want to reach out for it. How much further would it go before Noah realized all of this?

To his benefit, Noah knew his father better and how much it would be a pain to break the man's hold over Noah.

Noah seemed determined to burn his bridges with Mason and Ian. How in the hell was Brandon going to convince him to give up the ghost as it were and tell someone what happened in the barn?

Hopefully, before he burned any more bridges. It was pretty obvious Noah wasn't happy, and rightly so. Who would be in this situation? Noah's father was a cruel bully who terrorized Noah most of his life. It would be a long time before that kind of trauma could be realized and released.

Kind of like my family farm...

It had been a long time since Brandon thought about the farm his family owned. He had been looking forward to taking the reins from his father one day until the bank took the farm when his father could not come up with the mortgage for several months in a row. It had broken Brandon's heart, and since he had set up his life with the hope of one day owning the farm, it crushed his future.

When his parents moved, Brandon's father had set things up with Mason so Brandon could work on Dale Farm and still do the things he loved.

Brandon rolled down his window to enjoy some of the warm, gentle autumn air. Thinking about the farm always made him feel stuffy and hard to focus. Best to put those thoughts aside.

Brandon shifted his thoughts to Noah again. Somehow Brandon had to figure out a way to undo that programming. But how? Should he recommend therapy?

Noah mentioned during their only date that he had seen several therapists over the years.

Would any of them or a new one make any difference? Maybe he should talk to someone himself. He'd have to see. Meanwhile, he would look out for Noah to the best of his ability.

Having come to that conclusion, Brandon started back for the condo.

Chapter Ten

Noah glanced at his watch. It was about 5:30. He wasn't exactly sure when they all had dinner here, but at Dale Farm, dinner was strictly at six o'clock. Grammy tended to get upset if people didn't show up.

Where had Brandon gotten off too? Should he wait? It wasn't more than half an hour since they parted company. That man seriously needed to work on his temper. Didn't he realize Noah's anxiety hit the roof every time he blew his top?

Noah turned to the cabinet and started looking around at the available cookware. There was some pretty nice stuff. Grammy Carrie would love to have something like these. Many were high-class brand names.

Well, Daddy Caleb would only have the best. Noah wouldn't be surprised if the man had a mansion somewhere and no one knew about it. Noah had just placed a hand on a frying pan's handle when a guitar's musical notes filled the kitchen.

Was someone playing music? Luke, by chance?

Noah closed the cabinet and turned towards the archway that led to the living room. Caleb sat on the couch with an acoustic guitar resting on his lap. His fingers twisted the knobs, and he would occasionally strum the strings.

They let out a slight dinging noise several times, and he would adjust them again.

Caleb looked up as Noah approached. "Hey."

"Hi, Caleb. I didn't know you played the guitar."

Caleb snickered. "I'm full of surprises." After a beat, he asked, "Do you play?"

Noah shook his head. "I wish, but I never got a chance to learn. I sing a little, though. I'm not all that good."

Caleb's face lit up. "Oh really?" He strummed his guitar, sending a beautiful string of notes through the air.

"I'm not all that good, though." Noah's face fell, and he locked his gaze at his feet.

I hope he doesn't expect me to sing. Please don't let him ask me to sing.

"Well, I would love to hear you."

Noah took a step back. "Oh, I don't know."

"Look around. It's just the two of us here. Give it a try."

Noah took a deep breath and let it out. "Are you serious? You're going to make me sing?"

"Yes, boy. Sing for your supper."

"Okay, you asked for it. Do you know the song 'My Neverland' by Summer Warfield?

"I think so." Caleb made a few more adjustments to his guitar and started strumming the song's opening bars.

Noah cleared his throat. He'd missed his intro. *Damn, he's going to think I'm crazy.* "Uh, could you start over, please?"

"Sure." Caleb strummed the opening again, and Noah began singing on the beat.

"This is my home from home.

My playground of dreams,

Where recess never ends

And the sun throws off its beams

Darkness cannot impede

My childhood dreams.

I have found my neverland
My childhood sanctuary
I have found my neverland
Where I am free and safe
I found my neverland.
When shadows come to call
Life with all its cruelty
I return to my neverland
Where recess never ends.
My place of imagination
Where I began.
I have found my neverland
My childhood sanctuary
I have found my neverland
Where I am free and safe
I found my neverland."

When Noah finished singing, a round of applause filled the living room. Noah quickly looked around. Luke stood at the arch with a man with platinum-blond hair. Noah immediately recognized Drake, Luke's Pup. Brandon stood at the entryway, leaning against the wall with his arms crossed, a twinkle in his eyes.

Noah's face flushed with heat. When had they all snuck inside?

"Well, boy. You need some breathing lessons, but… Damn, you have a sexy voice." Caleb put his guitar aside with a playful smile gracing his handsome face.

Brandon crossed the living room and put his arms around Noah's waist. "I didn't know you could sing."

Noah smiled and blushed harder. "Neither did I, to be honest."

"Everyone is their own worst critic." Drake approached, followed by Luke, and both patted Noah on the back. "You did great. And I love that song."

"It was My Neverland by Summer Warfield. I really can't do her material justice."

"Nonsense. You're a diamond in the rough." Caleb smiled as he stood and stretched.

"Daddy Caleb, you have a phone call. Some lady from the office." Drake motioned back towards the kitchen.

Noah hardly noticed Caleb leave, as Brandon still had his arms around his waist.

Noah leaned in and kissed Brandon briefly on the lips. "I hope you're not still mad at me."

Brandon shook his head. "No, not really. But don't think I've changed my mind. I still think you're making a mistake, but despite that, wait..." he said when Noah started to interrupt. "Despite that, I love you and want to support you."

"Good, because I need to talk to you."

Luke cleared his throat and motioned for Drake to move upstairs. "We have some business to take care of right now."

"What business?" Drake turned his attention briefly back to Luke.

Luke cleared his throat, motioning with his eyes to Noah and Brandon and then back to the stairs.

"Oh, that business. Okay. I'll be in the Bastille." Drake headed for the stairs.

"Wait, I didn't mean… Drake?" Luke aimed for the stairs and then looked over his shoulders. "Silly pup." And then he disappeared at the top of the stairs.

The Bastille? Oh, I know what they'll be doing up there. Noah smiled inwardly as Luke and Drake disappeared upstairs.

"Great way to clear a room." Brandon let go of Noah and motioned for him to have a seat on the couch. "What's on your mind?"

"Well…" Noah took a seat beside him. "I wanna ask Caleb if he'll be my new daddy."

Brandon's mouth fell open. "Uh, I thought Mason was your daddy bear."

"He can't be anymore."

"You know I don't understand how this all works."

"I know."

"So, how are we a couple if you have a daddy?"

"You're still thinking monogamously. Is your heart so small you can't have more than one true love?"

"But aren't we primaries?"

That question buzzed around in Noah's head. Brandon and Noah, primaries?

"I wish I could say yes. I really wish I could, but I'm too broken to have a…"

Brandon put up a hand. "No, don't say it. You are a whole person, capable of love. You proved that in the barn before we even came here. You do deserve to be loved, Noah."

"I know."

"So, was that just sex for you?"

"What? No." Noah took a deep breath and slowly let it out. "Brandon, I care very dearly for you. But I don't know if I love you. I..." Noah took another deep breath. "Mark and Kelly, my so-called parents, messed me up pretty badly."

"I gathered that. Now let me finish."

Noah readjusted his feet and turned to face Brandon.

Brandon continued. "I know, and I understand. I do have feelings for you, Noah. I care about you, who you are, faults and all. I will wait however long it takes."

"Even if it takes forever?"

"Even if it takes forever."

Noah's heart began to swell, and he leaned over and pressed his lips against Brandon's.

Brandon put his arm around him and deepened the kiss.

Noah's heart beat harder, and his cock was beginning to respond to the attention.

Brandon pulled back, not letting Noah go. "Why Caleb?"

"Caleb is dating Mason. They are primaries. So if Caleb is my daddy, I can still spend time with Mason."

"If Caleb is your daddy, will he allow you to have a primary?"

"I don't know. It would be up to him."

"What about me?"

"What about you?"

"Could I be your daddy bear?"

Noah couldn't suppress a giggle, "You? A daddy bear?"

Brandon's face became a mask of irritation. "Yes, boy, me a daddy bear."

Noah bit his lip. Brandon's forceful dominance also went straight to Noah's dick. Noah shifted to accommodate for the growing discomfort.

"Do you even know what it requires? There's more to it than a couple of rolls in the hay."

"How so?"

"A daddy bear is responsible for his cub's health, safety, and well-being." Noah took a deep breath and continued, "It's very much like being a parent, just with a few added benefits."

"A parent?"

"Yes. The daddy bear's job is to raise his cub and ensure he is ready to be a productive member of society. They are also responsible for molding their character. Sometimes, sex can be used as a teaching device to make that happen."

Noah started to feel a tightness in his gut. Daddy Mason was such a sweet, gentle daddy. He was so kind and caring and thoughtful. That wasn't to say he wasn't above punishment if it was warranted.

God, Noah missed that man. Tears began to spring into his eyes. *Oh, God, what have I done?* The right thing. That was what he'd done. He had to protect Mason and Ian from Mark; if his absence was what that took, so be it.

Brandon pulled Noah into his arms, which felt warm and safe. Noah snuggled into them like a protective blanket.

"Thank you for everything you have done for me." Noah rested his head on Brandon's shoulder.

Brandon gently braced Noah's chin and lifted his lips to meet his for a kiss. A warm explosion filled Noah from the kiss. Noah held on to him tighter as the kiss deepened. Their tongues longed to continue exploring the insides of their mouths.

Brandon pulled away for a brief moment. "You wanna go upstairs?"

"Yeah," Noah muttered, unable to come up with better words. But that was all that was needed to convey the feelings. Noah wanted to make love to this man, and before the night was over, he was going to have him.

Brandon let go of Noah, and the two made their way to their room.

Chapter Eleven

When Brandon and Noah reached their room, Noah pulled off his shirt. Brandon followed suit.

"Brandon, will you please hold me?"

Brandon just nodded and patted the bed beside him.

Noah climbed up on the bed and snuggled his back into Brandon, who secured his arm around Noah's waist.

"I never realized my voice was so good," Noah said.

"Did you enjoy singing?"

"I did. Except for the applause. It was embarrassing." After a brief moment, Noah continued. "But exciting too. I didn't think I would like being put on the spot like that."

"Yeah, but you did, didn't you?"

"Somewhat."

"If music is something you think you'd enjoy, maybe you should pursue it."

"Oh, I don't know. Singing for friends is one thing. I don't know if I would be able to sing in front of a bunch of strangers."

"You don't think Summer Warfield or some other singers don't have stage fright sometimes?"

"Probably not as bad as mine."

Brandon learned into Noah, letting the scent of him fill and expand his senses.

Noah turned over to face him. Their faces were a few inches apart. Brandon locked eyes with him, drinking him in as much as possible.

"I'm still going to ask Caleb to be my daddy. Will you be okay with that?" Noah bit his lip.

"I'm not sure. I still don't quite understand this daddy-cub-thing world or how you can have multiple lovers."

Noah sighed. "It's not as hard as you think. I compartmentalize. I'll use the Dale Farm crew as an example."

"Okay."

"When Mason and I make love, he is teaching me and taking on the role of daddy. He may punish me if I do wrong or reward me with pleasure when I do right. Mason's job is to help me expand outside my box in and out of the bedroom."

"What about Ian?"

"Ian's my big bro."

"Wait, you call him 'big bro' even though you aren't related? Why?"

"Have you never had a friend you called a brother before?"

Brandon shook his head.

"That's too bad." Noah began to sound wistful.

Probably best to get Noah back on a different topic. "So tell me about Ian?"

Noah smiled. "Ian and I both claim"—he paused, frowned, and then continued—"claimed, past tense, Mason as daddy. So it was our ongoing joke that we were brothers, even though we aren't related." Noah put air quotes around the word brothers. "Because we share the same daddy. Make sense?"

"Not really, but I'll figure it out."

Noah closed his eyes and then opened them again.

"Honestly, Noah, I think you were happier with Mason. I don't think you're happy here."

Noah moved to speak, but Brandon reached up and touched his lips. "Just give it some thought before you make any decisions."

Noah kissed Brandon's fingertips. Their eyes locked for a moment before he leaned forward and kissed Brandon's lips.

Brandon braced Noah's head, deepening the kiss.

Noah groaned as his hand found its way to Brandon's back. Brandon let go of Noah's head and scooted over, pressing himself against him.

Noah kissed him hungrily and then turned to lie on his back.

Brandon moved as well, sliding nicely between Noah's knees. Feeling the more petite man trapped beneath him sent blood to all the right places.

Noah's pleading eyes locked with Brandon's. The hunger and need were starting to boil to the surface.

Brandon moved for a moment and rushed to get out of the remainder of his clothes. He glanced over. Noah was doing the same. They didn't need to speak at this point. Both knew what was in store and were hungry for it.

When they were both bare, they came together again. This time, Brandon took a lovely handful of Noah's ass.

Noah let out a whimper and moved his hips. "Mmmmm, please."

"Not yet," Brandon purred. He reached between Noah's legs and started stroking him. Noah let out a growl and began to grind himself into Brandon's hand.

"Damn, that feels good. Fuck." Noah closed his eyes, and his forehead hit Brandon's gently.

Brandon kept his hand where it was.

"God, if you keep that up..."

Brandon pulled away. "Not before I'm inside you." Brandon gently pushed Noah onto his back. He reached up and pursed Noah's lips with his fingers. "Get 'em all nice and wet for me, boy."

Noah sucked Brandon's fingers, and his tongue danced around them.

Brandon withdrew his fingers and started massaging Noah's opening. Noah let out a deep, primal moan.

God, the boy was sexy as fuck.

Brandon slipped the tip of one finger in, causing Noah to arch his back and groan loudly.

"Shh, boy, you don't wanna get the others in here, do you?"

Noah shook his head and then bit hard on the middle knuckle of his hooked index finger.

Noah's hole was so sensitive. Brandon looked up at Noah's face as he slid his finger back inside Noah's hole and pulled it out.

Back in again, with a bit of massage, and then back out again.

When Brandon added the second finger, Noah groaned and pushed down hungrily, wanting more.

By this time, Brandon was stiff, throbbing, and already dripping. If he didn't get inside Noah soon, he would blow.

"Ready?"

Noah growled out a rocky, "Yes, please, yes, now."

Brandon pressed his tool into Noah's opening then gently pushed the head into the sexy boy.

"Fuck!" Noah's eyes rolled back, and his head fell back on the pillows.

Brandon pulled out and pressed in again, a little farther, working all of his need into Noah. Every nerve in Brandon was on fire. He hoisted up Noah's legs, catching the back of Noah's knees with the crooks of his elbows so he came face-to-face with the boy he was growing to love.

Noah raised his chin, and Brandon caught him in a kiss as he started moving his hips. Each thrust brought a grunt from Noah around their kisses. Finally, Brandon raised his head, staring into Noah's eyes. Brandon knew at that moment he would do anything for those eyes. Eyes that had passed through him like Cupid's arrow since the day they first met.

Would Noah begin to see how much Brandon cared about him finally? How much he was willing to give up everything to make sure he was okay? His job, his life?

Brandon had known he belonged to Noah after that first kiss at the Rainbow Rose so long ago.

If only there were a way Brandon could get Noah to understand that.

Noah met each thrust with groaning and whimpering, which was sweet music to Brandon's ears.

"Fuck," Brandon groaned out. He could feel the tightness start below. A few more thrusts, and he pulled out, stroking himself to a messy finish right across Noah's chest to mingle with... Wait, was that cum already on Noah's stomach? Did he shoot already? Damn, he really must enjoy being a bottom.

Brandon slid in beside Noah and began kissing him, hard and fast, before it started melting into something gentler and comforting.

Noah buried his face in Brandon's chest, and Brandon kissed his forehead. "Fuck, that was hot."

Noah mumbled in agreement. Brandon wrapped Noah in his arms.

"I wanna try being your daddy, Noah, if you'll have me."

"Brandon..."

"Shhhh, wait. I need to learn what I'm doing, but I wanna be your daddy and take care of you, if that's what you need."

"I'll think about it, okay?"

"Take all the time you need."

Noah nodded and rested his head on Brandon's shoulder.

"Noah?"

"Hmmm?"

"Were you serious about asking Caleb to be your daddy? Can you have two daddies?"

"You could have as many daddies as you wanted, but it's easier to limit yourself to one, maybe two. But you will have to keep up with them both."

"Oh wow."

"Yeah."

"We can discuss it later."

"Okay."

Noah turned his head, and Brandon wrapped his arm around the man coming to mean so much to him.

"Noah, I wanted to tell you that..." Brandon noticed that Noah's eyes were closed and his chest rose and fell. "Noah?" the man was fast asleep. Brandon settled in and closed his eyes, breathing in Noah's spicy, sexy scent before he too fell asleep.

Chapter Twelve

Noah opened one bleary eye and then the other. Early morning light spilled into the room. A heaviness was upon him. It took him only a moment to realize Brandon's arm held him tight.

Sweet Brandon. Noah could quickly fall in love with him. Brandon was so patient and kind. Noah wished he knew why Brandon thought he was so special. Brandon deserved someone who wasn't so broken.

Noah dislodged himself from Brandon, carefully trying not to wake him.

Brandon let out a heavy sigh and turned over on his other side. It was as if losing Noah to hold had saddened him. His cobra-like back continued to rise and fall.

The pungent smell of coffee filled the air. Noah quickly hit the bathroom and dressed. Then he headed toward the kitchen.

Caleb was sitting at the table with a warm mug in his hands. In front of him was the morning newspaper. He looked up as Noah entered. "Good morning."

"Good morning."

"Did you sleep well?"

"Like the dead."

"Good."

"May I have some coffee?" Noah pointed at the coffeemaker.

"Sure, help yourself. Coffee mugs are in that cabinet." Caleb pointed at the cabinet over the drainboard.

Noah took a plain black mug, got some coffee, and doctored it with cream and sugar before taking a seat at the kitchen table beside Caleb.

Caleb cleared his throat and put down the paper he was reading. "Are you ready to discuss what happened at Dale Farm?"

Noah nodded as he took a sip of the rich-tasting coffee. He put his mug down. "First though, I have something to ask you."

"Oh?"

"Yes, sir." Noah swallowed once, and then took a slow deep breath. "I've been thinking about this for a while."

"Okay."

"I can't go back to Dale Farm because of some issues." Noah was sure this would be a ludicrous endeavor, but he had to try. It was probably the only way to save his relationship with Mason.

"Alright, start at the beginning."

Noah took a deep breath. "First, you have to promise me that you will not tell Mason."

Caleb shook his head. "I don't believe in keeping secrets from my primary."

"Oh..." Noah's face fell. "Okay, will you at least promise not to bring it up?"

"I'll do that, but if Mason asks me outright, I will tell him."

Noah let out a sigh. "I guess it will have to do." He took another sip of his coffee and went into everything. The hiring of Noah's father. Noah's history with Mark. The confrontation in the barn when Mark almost beat Noah, how Brandon saved him, and finally, Mark's threat.

As Noah told his story, Caleb kept stopping to clarify different things.

Finally, when Noah finished, his face felt warm and wet. Had he started crying? Noah wiped his eyes.

"You poor boy. No wonder you were terrified."

A lump started to form in Noah's throat. Unable to speak, he nodded and took another drink of coffee, hoping to wash down the lump. It didn't seem to work.

"So, what did you want to ask me? Did you want me to talk to Mason for you and explain everything? Or go with you to the police?"

"No. I have another question. Kind of a heavy one."

Caleb raised his coffee mug. "Well, spit it out, boy." He pressed the mug to his lips. *It's now or never, Noah, my boy,* came the thought from Caleb's eyes.

Noah closed his eyes, took a deep breath, and then opened them again. "Will you be my new daddy?"

Caleb choked on his coffee, carefully putting his mug on the table. Coffee had nearly gone everywhere. He grabbed a napkin and wiped his nose and mouth.

"Damn." Once he was settled, he turned to Noah. "What brought this on?"

"I've been thinking about it since I got here. You and Mason are primaries. I could stay here and still see Mason if you were my daddy. I love that man so very much. Also, if you were my daddy, Brandon would know I'm in good hands and can go back to work."

"Have you any idea what that would mean?"

"I've got a rough idea."

"Are you sure you can handle it? I'm not a gentle dom like Mason is. I can be very demanding. Ask Luke. Sometimes he has trouble dealing with me."

"But this is the only way."

"Short of just telling Mason the truth or calling the police."

God, no one was getting it. Noah bit his lip. Not even Caleb understood the reason for his fear of telling the truth.

"Will you at least think about it?" Noah bit his lip again and raised his eyebrows. "Please?"

Caleb let out a sigh. "I'll think about it. Meanwhile, I gotta get ready for work."

"Thank you, Caleb."

"Don't thank me yet, boy. I might just say yes." Caleb got up from the table and pushed in his chair. "Have a good day, kiddo."

"You too."

Caleb left the kitchen, And Noah finished his coffee and headed back upstairs. As he passed the open door of the Bastille, he heard laughter from inside, one of which was Brandon's voice. Noah knocked on the door.

"Come in," came Drake's rich voice.

Noah pushed in the door. Inside looked like a torture chamber from a horror film. However, none of the instruments in the room were meant for actual torture. A Saint Andrew's cross was set up against one wall. A sling was set up in one corner, with leather shackles at either end for wrists and ankles. Along one wall, various toys, tools, and crops hung, including but not limited to a cat o' nine tails, a couple of floggers, and several dildos.

Luke and Drake each had a dildo and were using them like swords.

"Hey, Noah." Brandon jumped up from his chair.

"What's going on in here?"

"We're discussing BDSM dynamics and Daddy Caleb, Drake's, and my dynamics."

"Really?"

"I'm still not one hundred percent sure. But I understand your relationship with Mason and Ian a little more."

Mason and Ian. Brandon meant Noah's past relationship with them. He felt wistful suddenly. For a moment, he would give anything for Mason to come stomping into Caleb's condo to whisk Noah back to Dale Farm. *Where do I belong?* No, that route was folly. He couldn't go back. Not while Mark was there.

Brandon pointed at Drake. "You are his pup, which means you are a dom?"

Drake shook his head. "No, I'm the sub. You see, the main dynamic is dominate and subordinate. The dom is in charge and barks orders to the sub, who follows through. The other dynamics are based on this power exchange. For example, there is master and slave, caregiver and child, handler and pet, etcetera." He pointed at Noah. "You know that Noah had a daddy dom?"

Noah frowned. "Well, I did."

"Okay, bear with me."

"Okay." Noah looked down at his feet. This was hard listening to Drake try to explain this.

"Daddy dom, boy sub," Luke chimed in at that moment. "Just like, handler dom/pet sub." Luke pointed to himself on the handler and Drake on the pet. "Our dynamic..." He pointed himself with his index finger and to Drake again with his thumb. "What we do is play out scenes where I'm the dog trainer and he's the pup in training."

"Woof," Drake barked out.

"Down, boy." Luke patted his head.

"Oh." Brandon's face lit up. "It's like role play. In the daddy dom/boy sub dynamic, the daddy is the parent and the sub is the child. Is that right?"

Noah grinned big. "Now you got it. Do you understand why Ian and I called each other big bro and little bro?"

Brandon nodded. "Yes. Because you are both Mason's subs. Mason being a daddy dom is shared between the two of you, so, as 'family,' a shared parent makes you brothers."

"Yes!" Noah threw his arms around Brandon and kissed him gently on the cheek.

"So, I got a question." Brandon pulled back a bit. So, what's a primary if Mason and Ian are your lovers?"

"Oh, that's a more complicated beast." Luke walked up to them. "A primary is your strongest, deepest romantic relationship. And as far as the outside world is concerned, they are your partner. So, technically, you are still single if you don't have a primary."

"So, primary equals boyfriend?"

"Right." Noah let go of Brandon. Thoughts of Mason's smiling face and gentle hands started flooding through Noah's mind, playing around with Ian, and gaming with him on occasion. God, he missed them all. If Caleb said yes, that would salvage that relationship, but what about Ian? He needed to work this out. How was he going to continue with Ian? And what about Brandon? How would he fit into the dynamic?

As primary? Maybe? He didn't seem to wanna give up. He definitely was determined. Noah had to give Brandon credit for that one.

Mason? Ian? Grammy Carrie, oh so kind, wise, and loving. Unlike his actual mother. *I miss them all. Damn you to hell, Mark, for doing this to me!*

Noah began to feel tears forming in his eyes. God, why did feelings have to hurt so bad? He tried to swallow the new lump in his throat.

"Earth to Noah…" Luke waved his hand in front of Noah's face.

"I'm sorry." Noah turned, headed out of the Bastille, and made a beeline for his room. He had to get away from the conversation. But could he run far enough away from his feelings?

"Noah, stop, please don't walk away."

Noah felt a pair of hands grab his shoulders. He froze as the hands slowly turned him around.

Brandon stood there with a look of concern. "Talk to me."

Noah shook his head, unable to find the words. He then started mumbling, "I miss them. Mason, Ian, Grammy Carrie, and even Rick. I wanna see them, but I can't."

Brandon pulled Noah into his arms. "I know, and I understand. It'll be okay. Somehow."

Noah wished he could believe that. He laid his hand on Brandon's shoulder.

How had his life become such a mess? What had he ever done to deserve such a monster for a father? Damn the bastard to hell!

"Shhhh, Noah, I got you. I got you."

Noah felt Brandon's arms circle him.

Why did Mark have to invade his neverland?

"No, Brandon. I'm not happy with the situation. But as long as that bastard is at Dale Farm, I can't be. I just can't."

"It's okay. I understand. But please understand that you can fix the problem. All you have to do is…"

"And here we go again." Noah wiped his eyes and pulled out of Brandon's arms.

"Noah. You have to take your power and self away from that man. You'll never be free otherwise."

Noah's nerves were fried. He needed some quiet time to think. Without a word, he did an about-face and headed off.

"Noah, please don't go."

Noah ignored him as he headed downstairs.

Chapter Thirteen

Brandon stared off in Noah's wake. Had he said something wrong? What was with Noah?

Brandon started making his way downstairs. The sound of running water met his ears, and he headed for the kitchen.

Luke was standing at the sink, filling it with water and dirty dishes. Drake was cleaning the stove.

"Hey, guys." Brandon nodded at the two of them as he entered.

"Hey, Brandon." Luke turned from his task. "Did you need something?"

"Is there anything I can do to help?"

"Sure. You can sweep and mop the floor." Luke pointed to a broom and dustpan.

"Okay." Brandon got them both and started sweeping.

While he swept, his thoughts drifted back to Noah. The man was being stubborn. Why was he letting his father have that power over him?

Brandon wasn't sure, but eventually Noah would have to confront him. This situation had to be resolved. But how?

Brandon moved the chairs out and started sweeping under the table.

Mason was unaware of who Mark was. If he only knew, he could do something, but as long as Noah kept a tight lip, nothing would change. What if Brandon took the initiative? Would Noah thank him for it? Should he tell Mason what was up? Then Mason could fire Mark, and Brandon and Noah could go home.

Noah would be back with the only family who ever truly loved him. The Dale Family. Noah wasn't very happy here. That much was obvious. All he did was mope and cry. He loved them all very much, and all this was killing him. Brandon didn't have to have a degree to see that.

"Earth to Brandon. Hello, dude?"

Brandon looked up into Drake's smiling face. "What?"

"You've been sweeping the same spot for several minutes." Luke turned from the sink, a dish in his hand. "Something on your mind?"

Brandon sighed heavily. "Noah, who else? Where is he, by the way?"

"Daddy Caleb took him out to a concert. They should be back in a few hours."

"Oh." Brandon bent down, swept up the pile he had formed, and emptied the dustpan into the trash.

"So..." Drake put down his towel, giving Brandon his undivided attention. "What's going on?"

"Noah's father was hired at Dale Farm. I caught him trying to beat Noah. The man is a psychopath. He threatened to harm everyone at the farm if Noah didn't leave."

"Abusive prick." Luke leaned his back against the counter. "So, that's why you guys came here."

"Yes."

Drake's mouth fell open. "Are you serious?"

Brandon nodded. "I'm at a loss as to what to do. I keep seeing signs that he wants to go back, but he won't open his mouth and say something. That man has Noah all twisted and bent over a barrel. I don't seem to be getting through to him."

Drake and Luke looked at each other then back at Brandon.

Luke Frowned. "According to Ian, Noah suffered his entire childhood. That kind of abuse takes along time to heal." He added under his breath. "If ever."

"Well, I gotta do something. I can't just sit here and let Noah burn all his bridges." Brandon sagged back in his chair, legs out. "The only thing I can think of is to tell Mason myself."

"That probably wouldn't be a bad idea." Drake pulled out a seat at the table. "Offer to be there with him. He needs your support right now. He may be more open to the idea."

Drake was right. If Noah had Brandon there when he talked to Mason, he might be more open to talking with the man. If anything else, Brandon could pick up and explain if and when Noah needed him to.

"I don't think it's a good idea. It should be up to Noah if and when he tells Mason." Luke put his hands on the table. "It isn't your place, if you stop and think about it."

"But, Handler, if they talk to Mason together, Noah may feel safer and more capable of confiding in his daddy bear." Drake rested his chin on his upturned hand.

Brandon buried his face in his hands. "Oh, I don't know. I can't seem to get through to him, try as I might. I feel like I'm banging my head against a brick wall."

"Well, give it a try and see how it turns out. He may be open to the idea. However..." Luke's sentence was cut off by a vibration from his pocket. He drew out his phone and tapped on the screen several times. "We have a visitor."

"Who?" Drake perked up.

"It's Ian."

"Uhhh..." Brandon froze. That man scared the hades out of him. He was probably here to see Noah.

About that time, the doorbell rang. Luke jumped up and headed for the door.

Drake and Brandon followed.

Luke pulled open the door to reveal Ian's large frame, arms crossed over his chest and an even bigger scowl on his face. "Hi Luke, is Noah around?"

"Uh, no. He's out with Daddy Caleb. Please come in." Luke stepped aside to let Ian into the condo. "Brandon's here, though."

As Ian entered, Brandon's skin started to crawl. He was dreading this visit. But would Ian be a good one to tell about Noah's father? Would he tell Mason so they could bring this drama to an end?

Also, would Ian be upset that he and Noah had been sleeping together? Did they still have something going on?

"Brandon, can we talk, please?" Ian started rocking in place, rubbing his hands along his crossed arms.

Seeing Ian like this wasn't doing anything for Brandon's nerves. Ian was unnerving at the best of times, despite Noah constantly calling him a marshmallow.

Brandon nodded to Ian.

"Don't mind us." Luke took hold of Drake's arm. "We have an appointment upstairs."

"We do?" Drake's confused face was quickly replaced with a sly smile. "Oh, yeah, we do." And he quickly followed Luke.

Brandon watched them as they disappeared up the staircase. He turned back to Ian.

"Okay, maybe you can tell me what the hell is going on here. Why did you and Noah leave the farm?"

Shit! This wasn't how he wanted to do this. Was Noah going to thank him for interfering?

"I was trying to protect Noah." That sounded a little less confident than Brandon had hoped.

"Protect him? Protect him from what?"

"More like...who."

"What?"

"Shit."

Brandon took a deep breath and slowly let it out. "Okay, you see, Mason..." The sound of the opening door cut him off.

"That was an amazing concert. See why I love Summer Warfield? She's terrific." Noah's excited voice filled the living area. "Thank you for taking me, Daddy Caleb."

"You're very welcome. I'm glad you had fun."

"Noah." Brandon raised his head with a sigh of relief. "Someone's here to see you."

Noah stopped and glanced over at Brandon. It took him a moment to seem to comprehend who was standing with him.

"Ian!" Noah threw his arms around the big man.

"Hello, little bro."

Suddenly, Noah's disposition changed. Slowly, he pulled out of Ian's hug. "You can't call me little bro anymore. I'm not with Mason anymore."

Ian looked dumbfounded and gave Noah a double take. "What do you mean, little..." Ian rolled his eyes impatiently. "I mean, Noah."

"I can't go back to Dale Farm."

Caleb turned to Brandon. "Maybe we should give these two a chance to talk."

"Good idea. Ian..." Brandon held up a closed fist. "Good to see you as always, man."

Ian did the fist bump. "Likewise."

Brandon turned to Noah. "I'll be up in our room if you need me."

Noah nodded.

Brandon followed Caleb into the kitchen to give the two a chance to talk.

Chapter Fourteen

Once everyone was out of the room, Noah's hackles went up. He knew why Ian was here, and it wasn't for a friendly visit.

Ian bit his lip and then started to speak. "So, Noah…"

Please don't ask why I left. Noah motioned for Ian to have a seat.

"I need to know what's going on, little bro."

"I wish I could tell you."

"Why can't you?"

"I have my reasons."

Ian covered his eyes with his hand and let out a frustrated growl. "Noah, can't you tell me?"

"I wish I could."

"Stop fucking wishing and do it."

"I can't."

"Why not?"

Noah began to feel tears of frustration roll down his face.

Instinctively, Ian reached out, but Noah pulled away. "No."

Ian drew back in shock. "Little bro?"

Noah held up a hand.

"No, little bro, I don't know what's going on with you, but it's nothing that can't be worked out."

"You don't understand."

"Then help me understand. Please."

Noah closed his eyes. They were going around in circles.

"If you want to know, I'll tell you. Something happened, and I can't go back now. Maybe sometime in the future, but I'm better off here right now."

"Noah." Ian's eyes sparkled with unshed tears. "Grammy misses you. I miss you. Daddy Mason misses you. Why the hell are you doing this? Did one of us do something to upset you? What, Noah? Please say something."

"I miss you all too."

Ian slapped his thighs and looked away quickly as tears spilled down his cheek.

Shit! There were many things that Noah could handle, but seeing the big imposing Ian cry was not one of them. He may be a large man but his heart was the gentlest, kindest one Noah had ever known. Seeing Ian cry was killing him.

Noah wanted to crawl under the couch and hide.

Ian wiped his eyes and turned back to Noah. "I guess you don't love us anymore."

"No, no, no. That's not true." Noah stomped his foot on the floor. "I love you all more than you know. Please, please, please don't make this harder than it already is. Just drop it. I'm here now and asked Caleb to be my new daddy."

Ian did a double take. His jaw went slack. It took only a few moments for him to finally find his voice. "You can't be serious."

"I am."

"Why? Mason's always been nothing but good to you since you first came to live with us. He has loved and spoiled you and..."

"Stop, Ian, please."

But Ian didn't respond but continued, raising his voice a little to speak over Noah. "He wants what's best for you. Do you know how awful it was when he came home the other day? That man was a wreck, and I thought he would collapse."

"Ian." Noah felt a lump form in his throat.

"You have reduced that strong, independent man to a shell of who he was."

Noah could see the trail of tears rolling down Ian's cheeks.

"Ian, please stop."

"Why should I, Noah?"

"Because you're breaking my heart."

"Like you broke Daddy Mason's heart? Like you broke my heart? Like you broke Grammy's heart?"

"Fuck you, Ian."

"Truth hurts, little bro, but I still love you."

Noah crossed his arms and turned away from him.

"Don't turn away from me."

Noah felt Ian's hands turn him back around.

"Don't you get it? I'm trying to protect you. I love you all so very much. You have all been more my family than my actual parents have been. I need to keep you all safe."

"Protect us? Keep us safe? What does that mean, Noah?"

"I can't tell you."

"I don't know what to do with you."

"Maybe you should leave."

"Fine."

"Is everything okay in here?" Caleb poked his head into the living room.

Ian and Noah both stood.

"Everything is fine. Ian was leaving." Noah sniffled and wiped his eyes.

Ian shot Noah a sad and angry look. "All this isn't necessary. Please give us a chance to fix what we did wrong."

"You didn't do anything wrong. Please understand that I'm trying to do what I feel is best."

"Best for who?" Ian tried to keep his voice level. Watching this display stung Noah deeply.

"I'm sorry."

"There's no need to be sorry. Just say something. We're asking that you talk to us and tell us what's wrong so we can fix it."

"I already fixed it."

"This isn't right."

Noah moved up and tried to put his arms around Ian's neck, but Ian caught Noah by the writs and pushed him gently away.

"No, not this time." Ian wiped his eyes again and headed for the door. He paused only a moment before he turned back to Noah. "I love you, Noah. If you need me, you know where to find me."

That hurt. Ian had never pushed him away before this. But wasn't that what he himself was doing? He was pushing everyone at Dale Farm away. First Mason, now Ian. Noah's heart fell into his stomach. "Ian."

Ian made it to the door and turned one last time to Noah. "I wish you luck, Noah. You will always be my little bro, no matter what. Please get whatever this is worked out as soon as possible. I'll miss you." Ian walked out, closing the door behind him.

Caleb came into the living room with Brandon close behind.

I can't let Ian go that easily. I love him too much, he's my big brother... Always. Noah made a beeline for the door. "Ian, Ian." His voice sounded dry and cracked and sore from crying.

Noah made it to the door just in time to see the elevator doors close on Ian, and then he was gone. Noah fell to his knees, tears streaming down his eyes. Must he lose everyone he ever loved?

Brandon came over and knelt beside him. "Noah, you knew this was going to happen. Your... I mean, Mark is abusing you even from so far away. And you're letting him get away with it."

"Oh, Brandon. I don't know what to do." Noah couldn't bear it. First Daddy Mason, and now his big bro. Damn Mark to every ring of hell for this.

Brandon climbed to his feet and held his hand out to Noah.

"You're going to have to tell them eventually." Caleb came over and also offered a hand.

Noah took both their hands, and the two helped him back to his feet.

"It would be better sooner than later." Caleb shot Noah a knowing glance and then headed for the kitchen. "Oh, Mason will be over later today." And he disappeared into the kitchen.

"Come on. Let's go grab some dinner somewhere." Brandon motioned for the door.

Noah wasn't sure he had an appetite, but he would try.

They enjoyed a quiet dinner out of the condo and returned an hour later.

When they got back, Mason's truck was in the parking deck.

Noah's heart soared but fell when he realized Mason was here to see Caleb, not him.

When they entered the condo, they were greeted by Luke and Drake.

"Is Mason here? I thought I saw his truck outside." Noah bit his lip.

"Yeah. He and Daddy Caleb are in the Bastille."

Noah sucked in his breath through clenched teeth. "Yeah, probably better to not disturb them."

"Yeah, because God only knows what punishment they would have in store for us." Drake had a playful smile spread across his lips.

"Down, boy." Luke patted Drake on the top of his head.

"Woof," Drake replied.

"I have an idea." Luke put his arm around Drake and hugged him tightly. "Why don't the four of us go to the Rainbow Rose for a drink? After the day we all had, that would be a good thing. Take the edge off."

Noah cringed. The Rainbow Rose, with that crowd? Was Luke out of his mind? He would be clinging to everyone. He would be terrified of touching anyone, even by accident. "Okay, but I'll be clingy. I don't do crowds well."

"It's okay. You can cling to me." Brandon took Noah's hand and placed it on his arm.

"Okay, it's set, then. You guys go get ready, and we'll—" Luke pointed at himself and Drake "—meet you down here in a little while."

Noah scribbled a quick note to Mason, asking him to stay until he returned. Maybe they were right. Maybe now would be a good time to tell Mason what was up. If Mark were serious about his threat, he would have done something by now. He put the note on the Bastille's closed door and headed to his room to get ready.

Chapter Fifteen

Noah clung to Brandon's arm as if he were the only life raft in the sea of people that crowded the Rainbow Rose. The large recessed dance floor was filled almost to capacity with dancers. High above the dance floor, people gathered on the balcony-esque second floor, some looking down at the dance floor, some talking and laughing.

Waves of techno music flooded the air to the point Noah could feel it in his chest.

How in the hell had he let them talk him into coming here? There were too many people.

It was so much easier here when Ian... Noah shut down that thought before it could complete. He couldn't think of Ian as his protector anymore. That chapter of his life was over.

The thought nearly sent tears streaming down Noah's face as he recalled his interactions with Ian earlier that day.

"Are you okay?" Brandon had stopped moving and covered Noah's hand with his own. Concern shined in his eyes.

"Yeah, I'm fine."

"What?" Brandon moved his ear closer to Noah's mouth. "I said, are you okay?"

"I'm fine," Noah lied. Why ruin everyone's night out by feeling anxious and depressed?

This place always brought out the worst in Noah. Except for the one time he got tipsy and first kissed Brandon. The memory brought a brief smile as Brandon escorted him to a nearby table.

The place wasn't overcrowded, as it had been on previous occasions. The last time they were here, everyone wound up with a bloody emotional nose over different run-ins they had. Noah had run into Brandon, Luke had bumped into an old friend, and poor Drake had gotten his heart broken in the worst possible way by his on-again-off-again boyfriend William. But being less crowded didn't mean his barriers weren't up. Noah was always cautious in a world where even an accidental touch could lead to a fist in the gut.

Noah took a seat with his back against the wall. Brandon got beside him while Luke took the other side, and Drake sat opposite Luke.

"Drinks are on me." Drake stood back up. "Brandon?"

"Beer."

"Noah?"

"Beer."

"Handler?"

"Whiskey sour, please." Luke raised his arms and stretched. "Thank you, pup."

Drake nodded. "Got it. I'll be right back." He disappeared into the crowd.

As Noah watched him go, he remembered the last time they had all gathered here—Luke, Drake, Ian, and himself. Drake's now ex-boyfriend William made them off again permanently by introducing his new girlfriend out of the blue. There seemed to be no love lost between the two of them almost immediately from the get-go. He remembered how Drake had cried for nearly an hour in the restroom and how he had lent Drake a sympathetic ear.

Noah turned to Luke. "Drake seems much happier now."

"Yeah, just as long as William and that bitch Charity don't show up, we should be alright."

A few moments later, Drake arrived with their drinks. After Drake passed them out, he sat back down beside Luke.

Drake had just gotten seated and taken a sip when Luke popped up. "Let's go dance. They're playing a slow one for a change."

"Mmmmm," Drake spoke around the edge of his glass, nearly spitting out his sip, before placing the glass on the table. "Okay." He got up and followed Luke to the dance floor.

Noah sighed, and he and Brandon looked at each other. What reason did they have for coming here again? Oh, yeah, give the daddy bears some private time. Lucky bastards, both of them. Noah could imagine what it would be like if he got caught between Daddy Caleb and Daddy Mason. He bit his lip and then turned back to Brandon. Brandon took a deep breath, and then his lips began to move.

Noah leaned closer. "What?"

"I said, do you wanna dance?"

Noah glanced at the dance floor. Nearly half of the dancers had vacated the floor when the slow song started. With more space on the floor, the feelings of claustrophobia wouldn't be nearly as bad, and Luke and Drake would be close, so it wasn't like he wouldn't have the support he needed if things went south. Noah sighed and nodded in response.

The two got up from the table and headed to the dance floor. As soon as they were close to Luke and Drake, Brandon put his arms around Noah's waist, while Noah put his arms around Brandon's neck.

After a moment, Noah wanted to pinch himself. Was he slow dancing with Brandon, or was this a dream? So close, their bodies were barely touching, their faces only inches apart. Noah just stared into those beautiful eyes. However, Brandon's attention seemed to be somewhere else. Was he staring at someone else? No, he couldn't be. Noah followed his gaze to an empty table close to the dance floor.

"Penny for your thoughts."

"Huh?"

"What's on your mind?"

"Just thinking about making love to your sexy self." Brandon looked away for a brief moment before he stared Noah back in the eye and smiled his radiant smile.

Somehow, Noah doubted that was what he was thinking. Noah didn't feel like pushing it. Brandon had been helpful and cooperative so far. Could he be giving up? Was that why he felt so distant?

Before Noah could finish his thoughts, Brandon leaned his head down and raised Noah's chin for a kiss. His lips pressed against Noah's, forcing them apart. His tongue invaded Noah's mouth, and Noah felt himself melt into the kiss.

Noah tightened his grip around Brandon's neck as Brandon deepened the kiss.

"Hot diggity damn!" Drake called out from a few feet away.

Both Noah and Brandon looked up. Noah's face was burning hot; he imagined it was a matching shade to Brandon's scarlet cheeks.

"Awww, knock it off." Luke smacked Drake on the shoulder.

Drake winced. "Damn, Handler." He turned to Noah. "Sorry, man."

Noah nodded in his direction. "It's okay." He turned back to Brandon, who was grinning like the Cheshire cat.

Noah smiled back at him.

Soon the song ended, and both couples moved from the dance floor with several other dancers. Some remained as a techno song came on, again flooding the place with its *thumpa thumpa*.

Noah sighed. At least he'd gotten a dance with Brandon tonight. But what had Brandon been thinking? He'd seemed so lost in thought through most of the dance. Well, until the kiss. Maybe he *had* been thinking about making love to Noah. The thought sent a spark through Noah that went straight to his dick. He bit his lip, trying to calm the sensation. The thought of that man inside him was almost too overwhelming for him to bear.

Could the two of them make the primary relationship they were forming work? Because from the looks of Brandon at the moment, Noah was beginning to wonder. Maybe he was taking all this way too far. No, that wasn't true. He needed to stay away from Mark. If Mark got his clutches on him again...

Noah killed the thought before he could complete it. He knew how it would end, and putting an image to it wasn't going to help his nerves.

Luke pulled out his phone, tapped it once with his finger, and put it to his ear. Almost immediately, he plugged his other ear and motioned that he would be right back. He walked off towards the bathrooms and the bar.

"I wonder who that could be?"

"Probably Andy. He's been calling Luke for the last couple of weeks." Drake stared off in Luke's wake.

"Andy?"

"Andy Jones. He's a friend of Luke's from college. I don't know him very well, though." Drake shrugged.

"Oh." Noah nodded.

After a few moments, Luke returned to the table. He pocketed his phone and put his hands palms down on the table. "The daddy bears say it's time to return to the condo. Mason's still there, Noah."

Noah's heart raced. *It's now or never, Noah. Now or never. Either tell Daddy Mason the truth, or let him go forever.* Noah bit his lip. He couldn't believe he was doing this. All that fear of Mark and what he could do. Would Mark follow through with his threat if Noah told Mason the truth?

Perhaps they would be able to have the cops present when Mason fired his ass to make sure that everything stayed safe and calm. The man had broken the law, and it was time he paid for his crimes. He did time in prison once. Noah would not be overly heartbroken if the man had to go back for a long time.

"Brandon and I need to get back. I have to talk to Mason. It's important."

"Okay, let's go." Drake climbed to his feet, and Noah and Brandon followed suit. After a few moments, they were on their way back to the condo.

* * *

Brandon chanced a glance at Noah. Was this going to happen? Was Noah finally breaking down and telling Mason the truth and ending this terrible situation? Back at the condo, Brandon's mind was flooded with thoughts of Noah and making sure they would be able to return to the farm. Noah missed everyone so much; this was the only way to make that happen.

When they finally reached the condo, Brandon's heart was pounding in his chest. Inside the living room, Caleb was reclined on the couch with Mason snuggled into his arms. Mason sat up as they entered.

"Daddy Mason," Noah cried and went to embrace Mason.

Mason took Noah into his arms. "You had something you wanted to talk to me about?"

"Yes, I do. Daddy Caleb, may we use the Bastille so we can talk in private?"

"Be my guest." Caleb motioned towards the stairs with his hand.

Mason and Noah then headed upstairs.

Luke and Drake sat on the couch next to Caleb, and Brandon began to pace. Finally, this was all going to come to an end. Mark would get fired, Brandon would be able to get back to work, and *finally*, Noah would be back with Mason and Ian.

"*Ugh*! Brandon, would you please sit down? You're making me dizzy." Caleb motioned to an overstuffed chair on the other side of the living room.

"I'm sorry, Mr. Olivera. I'm just nervous."

"Noah told me what happened that brought you guys here."

"He did? What exactly did he say?"

"He told me about his father. Is that what he wants to talk to Mason about?"

"I sure hope so." After a moment, though, Brandon quickly spoke up again. "Not that I don't appreciate everything you have done for Noah and me, but I really wanna go back home to the farm."

"Yeah, and I know Noah does too. He's not been one hundred percent happy here, and we all know it."

God, what Brandon would give to be a fly on the wall. *Please, please, please let Noah finally break down and tell Mason the truth. If he doesn't, though, I'm stepping in. Enough is enough.* Noah needed to be back on Dale Farm, where he was happiest. And if he didn't see that, he was going to. But the question was, if Noah didn't tell Mason and Brandon Did, would Noah forgive him for going against his wishes?

Well, there was only one way to find out. Brandon stood and started for the stairs, but Caleb jumped up and blocked his path. "No, let the two of them talk."

"This is driving me crazy."

"I know, but you need to give them time to work things out."

About that time, Mason came walking down the stairs without Noah. His face looked crestfallen again. Had Noah even told him the truth? From the look on Mason's face, Brandon was guessing not.

That's it. I've had it.

Caleb stood aside to allow Mason to come down the stairs. "Everything okay?"

"No. He still won't say anything to me."

Fuck! Okay, time to put this nightmare to an end. "Mason?" Brandon reached out to his boss. "Can I have a word?"

"I guess. You can walk me out." Mason kissed Caleb and headed for the door. Brandon followed.

Once the door was closed, Mason asked, "What's going on here, Brandon? I'd be happier if someone would tell me."

"You mean Noah didn't say anything?"

"Nope. Tell me."

Brandon took a deep breath. This was for Noah's own good; if he couldn't do it, it was up to Brandon. Hopefully, things would work out for themselves after this. Hopefully it wouldn't end things with Noah. Hopefully...

"Speak up, Brandon."

Brandon cleared his throat. "I know what's going on with Noah."

"What? Tell me."

"Do you promise not to tell Noah I told you?"

"I promise nothing. Now tell me."

It was now or never. "His father."

"What?"

"His father. You hired his father, Mark, as a new farmhand."

"Wait a minute. The man who abused Noah?"

"Mark Jennings, the man you hired, is Noah's biological father. I caught him in the barn about to beat Noah had I not shown up." Brandon cringed.

"What the fuck? Tell me everything. *Now*!" Mason's face had twisted into a mask of anger and regret. "Don't leave out any details."

Oh, my God, Brandon, you are a dead man. Noah's going to kill you.

Carefully lowering his voice, Brandon told Mason everything about how they were making out in the barn, how Mark had cornered Noah and nearly beaten him. How Brandon had saved him from Mark and the two fled the farm.

As Brandon spoke, Mason's face grew darker and darker, leaving Brandon to wonder if the man wasn't going to stroke out. When Brandon finished, Mason only made one comment, "I'll kill that son of a bitch," before he turned to go back into the condo.

Brandon grabbed him by the arm. "Please don't tell Noah I told you. He's going to be pissed."

"Well, I'm pissed off. Why didn't someone come to me?" Mason pulled his arm free.

Dear God, he was strong. Before Brandon could say another word, Mason went back into the condo. As the door closed, Brandon could hear him say, "Where's Noah?"

You've gone and done it now, Brandon, my boy. Now Noah will never forgive you. Heavy-hearted and miserable, Brandon decided a walk was in order and turned away from the condo's door.

Chapter Sixteen

Mason thundered into the room. His blood was boiling with anger. "I wanna talk to the two of you in private right now." He glared at his primary and cub.

Noah looked like he was about to faint. His face had gone so white. Mason took several deep breaths and tried to calm his mood.

Caleb escorted them upstairs to his bedroom. Mason had seen the room several times with his full king-size bed, still disheveled from their session earlier that afternoon. Noah entered first, followed by Caleb.

Mason put his finger right square in the middle of Caleb's chest. "You knew damn well what was going on, didn't you?"

Caleb's face fell. For the first time since his mother's heart attack, Mason saw shame and guilt in Caleb's eyes.

"Yes, I knew. Noah told me."

Mason turned to Noah. "You could tell everyone else but me what was going on? Why the hell didn't you come to me, boy?"

Noah shied away and took a seat on the bed.

"Come on, speak up, boy."

"What do you know?"

God, Mason hated this.

"I know your father came to work on the farm as a farmhand."

"Who told you?"

"That doesn't matter. What matters is why the hell didn't you tell me? I would never have hired that son of a bitch."

"I couldn't tell you."

"Why not?"

Caleb moved to step between Noah and Mason, but Mason sidestepped him. "This is between Noah and me. You've done enough." Mason noticed Caleb's face twist up with annoyance, but he ignored his primary.

"Mason. He was scared out of his wits the night he came here. It would be best if you gave him some understanding. You don't know what he's—"

Mason held up a hand. "I'll hear it from Noah, thank you."

Noah was white as a sheet. "It was Brandon who told you, wasn't it?"

"It doesn't matter how I found out. Why didn't you say something?"

"He threatened me."

"What?"

"Mark. He threatened to burn the house down with everyone inside if I didn't leave or if I told anyone." Noah burst into tears. "He would have beaten me again in the barn if Brandon hadn't shown up and saved me."

Mason just wanted to hold the boy, but first, he needed to get through this.

"Is that the reason you left? Because of him?"

"Yes."

"That dirty son of a bitch!" After a moment, the irritation that had flooded Mason began to slowly subside. He reached out, taking Noah into his arms. "Oh, my dear boy. I wish you had said something. I would have fired him on the spot and called the police."

Noah laid his head on Mason's shoulder. Mason just held him. Mason remembered holding Noah just like this when the news came about James. Noah had been closer to James than he had been to Mason and Ian before James's death. It had hit him hard.

Noah looked up. "Daddy Mason, will you ever forgive me for causing all this grief?"

Mason bit his lip, and tears started to form in his eyes. The teary-eyed stars in Noah's eyes were almost too much for Mason to bear. His poor boy. *His* poor boy. Unable to speak, Mason nodded. Finally, he said, "Oh, Noah. There's nothing to forgive." He lowered his head and, using a finger, raised Noah's lips to meet his own. He parted from Noah and continued, "I will always keep you safe, but you have to open your mouth and say something next time you feel like you're in trouble. Promise me?"

Noah nodded. "I promise. Oh, Daddy Mason, I've missed you something terrible." Noah threw his arms around Mason and kissed him again. This time, Mason cupped the back of Noah's head and deepened the kiss. Then it was Noah's turn to pull away. He turned to Caleb.

"Dadd... Caleb. I want to thank you for everything you've done for me. I'm sorry, but I have my daddy. I don't think I'll be one of your cubs."

"Who said so?" Caleb turned to Mason. "Mason and I are primaries, so technically, we're both your daddies."

"You mean that?"

Mason had to agree. They *were* seeing each other now, so technically, they *were* both his daddies. Mason nodded.

Noah threw his arms around Caleb next and kissed him. Caleb slid his hands underneath Noah's shirt, slowly bringing it up over his head and revealing his bare chest. Noah turned and pressed himself against Mason. "Show me how much you love me, Daddy. Please."

Mason smiled at the boy and slowly ran his hooked index finger along his sparsely hairy chest. Noah's eyes rolled back with pleasure, and he unbuttoned Mason's button-down shirt.

Caleb was already unbuttoning his shirt. Noah's eyes went wide as he scanned Caleb's bare, muscular, hairy chest. "Damn."

Caleb grinned big and stepped forward. Mason and Caleb sandwiched the boy between them. Each one picked a shoulder and kissed the nape of his neck. Noah moaned out in ecstasy. With lips and hands smoothing the boy's body, each man had his thoughts to share.

I will always protect you, Noah, no matter what, Mason's hands said as they slid over the boy's chest and found their way to his jeans. He unfastened them and let them fall to the ground. He moved just a bit to allow Noah to step out of them, and Noah stepped and kicked them away. Noah began pulling on Mason's pants but seemed to have trouble unfastening them. Mason took a moment to undo them and kicked them away, revealing a simple pair of white briefs, his prominent bulge outlined beneath the fabric.

Noah took his hand, cupped that bulge, and began rubbing it, sending tendrils of pleasure coursing through Mason. Mason put his arms around both Noah and Caleb. Caleb was already turning Noah towards the bed. As Noah lay on his back, Caleb slid in beside him. Mason took the other side, letting his hands roam over the boy's body.

"Daddy loves you, boy. He's been so worried."

"I know, Daddy Mason. I've missed you all too, so very much."

Noah went straight for Mason's nipple. He knew how to get his daddy all hard and stiff. He started sucking on that small nub. Mason's head rolled back with Noah's ministrations.

He watched as Caleb caressed Noah's side. Mason slowly pulled away and turned Noah to face Caleb and give him his turn. The look in Caleb's eyes said it all as he made love to Noah.

He's our boy!

He's our boy, Mason's eyes returned.

We will protect him always.

He will always feel safe with us.

No one will ever be cruel to him again.

Never.

Noah turned back to Mason. "I wanna ride you. Take me, please."

"Okay, Noah, whatever you need. I will always be here for you."

Noah mounted Mason and slid Mason's hot, throbbing cock inside himself. The feeling of tightness went straight to Mason's head. He smiled gently up at Noah as he took hold of Noah's waist and guided the young man up and down.

"Fuck, that feels so good. I've missed this." Noah's eyes closed as he took Mason inside him.

"I missed you too, boy. Please don't leave again."

Noah ran his hands up and down Mason's chest. *My God, his hands.* Mason sucked in a deep breath and slowly let it out.

His body was telling him what to do. He guided Noah up and down on his cock, using the boy as a masturbation toy.

"God, Daddy, I've missed you so much." Tears had begun to form in Noah's eyes. "Promise I will trust you to look out for me from here on out."

"We both will." Caleb's voice was soft and gentle. It seemed out of character for the shrewd businessman.

Noah glanced at Caleb then back at Mason. He leaned down and kissed Mason, pressing his tongue into Mason's mouth. Then, after coming up for a breath, he got off Mason and mounted Caleb.

"Thank you for looking out for me. I'm so sorry to have burdened you the way I did."

"No need to apologize, boy. You are safe, and we'll always keep you safe. You just have to tell us you're in trouble."

"I promise I will from now on."

Mason watched as Noah took Caleb deep inside. The sight of Caleb taking his cub was almost too hot to handle. He looked downward to ensure he hadn't shot his load yet.

Still dry as a bone.

Mason began stroking himself as he watched Noah ride Caleb. He'd never imagined that his primary could be so gentle and loving. It had been rough and rowdy the last few times they had made love. At the same time, Mason liked that it. He also liked the gentleness, the intimacy. Perhaps it was something he could talk to Caleb about later. Right now, though, they needed to focus on Noah and each other.

Caleb's face was so red, setting off his amber-colored eyes. His teeth were clenched together as his hands caressed Noah's body. Noah's head was back, groaning out in pleasure each time he impaled himself on Caleb's thick cock. Caleb then held Noah above him and started pounding him from underneath.

"Take me, Daddy Caleb. Take my hole."

This seemed to drive Caleb even crazier, and he lost his gentile nature, almost immediately getting rough with Noah.

Mason began to worry that he might get too aggressive, but Noah seemed to enjoy himself. The pleasure spreading across his face was almost too much for Mason to bear, and he stopped stroking himself. Damn, it was hot watching Caleb take his boy. *Their* boy.

Suddenly and without warning, Caleb's face began to contort. He thrust into Noah one more time before his face twisted into a mask of ecstasy and he reached his climax. Noah dismounted with a grunt and kissed Caleb long and deep. He then turned to Mason and remounted him.

It didn't take Mason long to reach his climax. Within moments, he shot his load.

Noah collapsed on Mason and started kissing him deeply. Mason's heart was beating hard in his chest. He almost couldn't breathe from the weight of the more petite boy. But he kept sucking in the air. He gently turned himself and Noah on their sides.

Caleb wrapped an arm around them both.

"I'm your boy, Daddies. I trust you to keep me safe always." Noah bit his lip as he looked at one of his daddy bears and then the other.

"We will always keep you safe, Noah." Mason started brushing Noah's hair out of his face. "You will always be our boy, no matter what."

Mason knew at that moment that what he said was true. When he returned to the farm, Mark Jennings or Easton was going to be history. He was going to make sure the police are called. No one, but no one messed with his boy. He'd be lucky if Mason didn't beat the hell out of him for terrorizing his boy. His and Caleb's boy. There was going to be hell, and he was ready for it.

For now, though, he watched as Noah's eyes began to get droopy. Caleb looked over Noah's shoulder at Mason. He mouthed the words, *Poor boy's exhausted.*

Mason returned his primary's comment with a grin and a slight nod. Well-deserved exhaustion.

"Noah?" Mason glanced at his boy.

"Yeah, Daddy Mason?"

"I love you." He kissed Noah's forehead.

"I love you, too, Daddy Mason. I promise I'll never run away again."

"If you do, Daddy's just going to chase after you again and again."

"Mmmm, thank you, Daddy," Noah mumbled.

"You're welcome, boy." Mason kissed his forehead again.

Noah closed his eyes, and his breath became shallow. Poor kid was tuckered out from everything, emotionally and physically. Perhaps the best thing for Mason and Caleb to do was talk about what to do.

"Caleb?"

"Yes?"

"I have a favor to ask. I know it's a lot, but..."

"Name it, and it's yours."

"Can Noah stay with you another night or two? I need to go home and deal with this."

"Sure, no problem."

"Thanks."

"Anything for our boy." Caleb put his arm around Noah and spooned him.

"You're the best."

"I try."

The two men then snuggled into their boy and also found their dreams.

Chapter Seventeen

Noah woke from his brief snooze.

The daddy bears were both out cold.

He untangled himself as carefully as possible from the two of them and climbed out of bed. His bladder felt like it was going to burst. He used the bathroom attached to Daddy Caleb's room to relieve himself, returning to get dressed.

Noah slipped on his shirt. Did Brandon tell Mason what was going on? Why did they have to talk out in the hallway? Was that what happened?

Mason moaned out. Noah froze and looked back at the bed. He didn't want to wake the daddy bears. Mason just stretched and snuggled up to be a little spoon to Caleb. Neither of them noticed he was gone, and that was a good thing for now. Noah had to find Brandon and get some answers before Mason left.

Now, where could that man be? Noah started upstairs and checked the Bastille. No one was there. Then he checked the bathroom out in the hall. Nope, not there either. Bedroom?

Noah glanced into the room, and Brandon sat on the bed with his face in his hands. As Noah entered the room, Brandon looked up. "Hi."

"Hi."

"What's up?"

Feelings of hurt began to well up in Noah. He had planned to open up and tell Mason about Mark, but he'd needed more time to make sure it was the right decision, but Brandon had broken his trust and beat him to it. How could he have done such a thing? He knew that Mark… Oh, what was the point now?

"Nothing." Noah couldn't hide the frustration from his voice. He turned away from Brandon and pulled off his shirt. It was late, and he was exhausted.

"Noah, I can tell something's wrong. You sound upset. Please talk to me."

Noah bit his lip. He didn't want to have this conversation now, but it didn't seem like Brandon would let it rest. "Mason knows."

"Oh?" Was that nervousness in Brandon's voice? He was trying to play it cool. He seemed to know he did something wrong. Good. He needed to feel miserable for a while.

"Mason knows that Mark is my father. He knows everything. I only told you, Caleb, Luke, and Drake. So one of you had to have told him."

"I…" Brandon stood and tried to put his arms around Noah, but Noah moved away.

"I'm going to ask you. Did you tell Mason, even though I begged you not to?"

Brandon let out a sigh, and his gaze fell to the ground. His silence was all the answer Noah needed.

How could Noah fault Brandon for telling Mason the truth? But then, the road to hell was paved with good intentions, so Kelly always said.

"I just…"

"No. I just can't with you right now." Noah held up a hand. "I'm exhausted, and I wanna go to bed."

"Okay."

Noah pulled off his socks and climbed into bed in only his jeans. He pulled up the covers and turned his back to Brandon, folding his arms over his chest. How could Brandon do that to him? He had planned to tell Mason. He loved everyone at Dale Farm and wanted to return so badly. He was willing to stand up to his father for all of them. Even though Brandon had done what Noah couldn't. It still bothered him that Brandon had taken that opportunity away from him no matter when he would have told Mason.

"Noah, please let me explain. I was trying to help."

"Stop already, would you? Mason knows." Noah rolled over to face Brandon. "To be honest, I'm somewhat relieved and terrified at the same time. I'm terrified that Mark will follow through on his threat."

"Well, now that Mason knows, he can call the police and deal with Mark properly. Hopefully, things will be able to return to normal."

Normal? When was this family ever normal? Noah sat up in bed. "I don't think there is such a thing as normal."

Brandon sighed. "Get some rest, Noah. We can talk more tomorrow."

Noah turned back onto his side away from Brandon and let exhaustion take over.

* * *

Noah awoke slowly, with a realization. I forgive him. He rolled over bleary-eyed and reached out his arm. But he kept reaching, feeling nothing but sheet and air. He quickly bolted upright in bed. "Brandon?"

But the bed was empty.

Noah swung his legs over the edge of the bed and sat up. "Brandon?" He stood, dressed only in his jeans. He turned on the side lamp and looked around the room. There was no sign of the man he'd called for at all. "Brandon?" Something was different. Noah pulled on a shirt and looked closer around the room. It took him only a moment to realize that Brandon's stuff was gone. His keys, his wallet, everything.

Noah walked over to the window. He saw Brandon's truck heading out from the parking garage and pulling up to a stop light. "*Brandon!*" Noah raced out of the room, along the hall, and down the stairs. He nearly slipped on the last few and leaped to stop himself by catching the banister. He turned into the living room and found the closed door. By the time he reached the front door, he had realized the light had probably changed and Brandon was long gone. His heart sank into his stomach. Where was he going? Would he be back? He needed to talk to him.

"Noah, is that you?" Luke's voice called from the kitchen.

"Yeah." Noah headed for the kitchen.

Luke sat there with a drink in front of him. He was dressed in nothing but a pair of pajama bottoms. His strawberry-blond hair was disheveled.

"He's gone."

"What?"

"Brandon." Luke took a sip of his drink and motioned for Noah to sit down.

Noah pulled up a chair and took a seat next to Luke. "What do you mean, he's gone? Where did he go?"

"I don't know. Probably back to Dale Farm."

"But why?"

Again Luke shrugged. "He just asked me to give you this." Luke handed Noah an envelope that had his name handwritten on it.

Noah took the envelope and tore it open. Inside was a folded piece of notebook paper. He carefully unfolded it and began to read.

Dear Noah,

I did tell Mason, and I am not sorry. I did it for you because I would rather be lonely while you're happy than you miserable with me. Your daddies will love and care for you now. I love you, Noah Easton. Always have and always will. I hope one day you can see I did this for your good. I hope one day you will forgive me.

With love,
Brandon

Noah's eyes filled with tears. "But dammit, I forgave him." He took a deep breath and slowly let it out, bringing his hands up to his face. "Can I ask you a favor?"

"Sure."

"Will you take me to Dale Farm? Please?"

"Yeah, I can take you tomorrow. I'm not doing anything special. I'm sure Drake and I can do that while Daddy Caleb is at work."

Noah nodded. He had to talk to Brandon. It was the only way they were going to work this out. "I wish I could go now."

"I know, but it's late, and everyone there is probably asleep."

"I'm just worried about what Mark will do if he finds Brandon there."

"I know, but there's not much we're going to be able to do about it tonight." Luke took another sip of his drink. "Not only that, but I've been drinking. I don't think you want me driving. Also, I think Daddy Caleb may stay home tomorrow to go with you to Dale Farm."

"Fair point. Can I join you, please?"

"Help yourself. Rum is in the cabinet, and the cola's in the fridge."

Noah made himself a drink and sat with Luke.

"I think I love him."

"Oh?"

"Yeah."

"I could have told you that."

Noah turned and shot Luke a raised eyebrow. Then he put his arms and head down on the table. Damn it, if he didn't love Brandon and he'd just let him slip right through his fingers. "Oh my fucking God! I'm an idiot!"

Before Luke had a chance to make a smart-ass remark, Noah raised a single finger in the air. "Don't say it. Whatever you're thinking, don't say it."

Luke just sighed. "What I was going to say was, things aren't irreparable. You guys just had a miscommunication. You need to talk to him and work things out. Just trust in your gut. Tomorrow, we'll take you to Dale Farm, and you can deal with your father and work things out with Brandon."

He was right. Noah felt somewhat rested but not by much. It had been a very long day. But at least now, things were going to change. Maybe he could go back to Dale Farm, where he belonged. Back to Daddy Mason, Ian, and Grammy Carrie. It would be so lovely to see them all again.

Did he do this because he thought it was best? There was no way of knowing until Noah got the chance to talk to Brandon.

"I'm heading to bed." Luke stood up from the table and stretched.

"I'll be heading up there soon."

"As you wish." Luke disappeared through the arch.

Alone with his thoughts was probably a bad idea. Noah finished off his drink and headed upstairs to his room.

It seemed so empty now, without Brandon next to him. How long had they been here? Eight or nine days? In that time, he'd nearly destroyed everything he had come to love. His relationships with Mason and Ian. He nearly destroyed the beautiful love that had blossomed between him and Brandon. Brandon probably left because he felt ashamed of having told Mason the truth of the matter, despite Noah's begging to the contrary. He should have been furious at Brandon, but with the thought of that kind, sweet, gentle man who was there and saved him, Noah couldn't be angry at Brandon. Especially if he thought he was doing the right thing.

Noah pulled off his clothes and climbed into bed. At least tomorrow, they'd have a chance to talk and work things out after Noah dealt with that bastard who did all this to him. *God help me to survive tomorrow. So much is riding on what happens when I return to the farm.*

Chapter Eighteen

Brandon pulled his truck up the long drive to the farm. His arms hurt, his head was heavy, and his heart was in his stomach. How could he have broke his promise to Noah and told Mason? Noah seemed so resentful and hurt over all of this. What the hell had Brandon been thinking?

A curtain of dust followed the truck as it made its way to the two-story Victorian house. Noah used to say it looked like a gingerbread house. Something he picked up from Mason over the years, Brandon supposed.

Brandon parked the truck and climbed out. His nerves were on edge. Would Mason let him have his job back? There were bound to be questions about Noah. Was he safe? Where was he now? Was he coming back? How much did Mason tell everyone about what was going on?

There was only one light on in the house. So someone had to be up. As he climbed out of his truck, an orange light appeared and disappeared from the porch. He sat on the porch swing, a cigarette in his hands. Wow, Mason was smoking again. Brandon thought that he had quit. What was this all about anyway?

"Good evening, Brandon. Welcome home."

"Thank you."

"Noah is...?"

Brandon looked around. "Right where I left him. You know where."

"Good." Mason took a drag off his cigarette and then crushed it out in a can that he had in his hand. "I would like to talk to you about your job."

"You didn't give it away, did you?"

"No, it's still available. I'm not a cruel, heartless man, Brandon. I know you left to help Noah. And that means more than anything to me."

"I'm sorry about leaving you down one man, but I... Wait, what?"

"You saved Noah, and that means a lot to me. He is very special and dear to me. You understand that."

"Yes, I understand. I would never do anything to hurt Noah. I love him very much."

"Good, because he's still my cub. I know how much you care about him."

Care about him? Damn, I love Noah. Brandon was about to come up on the porch when the porch light came on and Carrie Dale stepped out.

"Brandon, you're back. Did you enjoy your vacation?"

"Vacation?" He glanced at Mason, who just looked off into the distance. "Not really, but it's good to be back. Where is everyone?"

"Ian's upstairs on his computer," Mason answered. "Rick and Mark are in the bunkhouse. Why don't you join them, and we'll meet up tomorrow morning."

"No, Brandon, wait. Have you eaten yet?" Carrie stepped forward.

"No, I haven't eaten since lunch. I missed dinner at..."

Mason stopped him from speaking by placing his finger to his lips. He mouthed the words, *The night has ears.*

He had to be talking about Mark. He must be somewhere nearby. Brandon nodded in acknowledgment before speaking again. "No, I skipped dinner like an idiot. May I get something to eat?"

"Of course. Come in, and we'll see what we can find." Carrie motioned for Brandon to follow her into the kitchen, and Mason followed behind him.

Once they were in the house, the politeness dropped and Carrie turned to Brandon.

"Noah is safe, right? He still at..." She motioned to a point in the distance.

Brandon nodded. "Where's Mark?"

"He's with Rick at the bunkhouse playing cards and having a few beers. We've planned to let him spend the night, and then I'll be dealing with him in the morning." Mason took a seat at the table and motioned for Brandon and Carrie to do the same.

"Once we deal with Mark, then Noah can come back. I can't believe I was so stupid." Mason turned to Carrie, who had put her hand on his shoulder.

"This isn't your fault. You didn't know who he was when you hired him. How would you know that he was going to go after Noah? It was just a bad coincidence." Carrie took a seat at the table.

"I don't know what I'm doing to do for the night. I can't go back to Caleb's, and if I go to the bunkhouse, he'll know something's up." Brandon put his hands on the table, palms down.

"That's easily fixed." Carrie glanced at Mason. "He could crash in the main house for tonight on the sofa. Then Mark won't be the wiser that something's amiss." After a brief pause, she continued. "I knew there was something odd about that man."

"Well, we'll take care of him and get Noah back with us. Meanwhile, you better get some sleep. Tomorrow's going to be a difficult day."

"Let's get some food and get you settled for the night. Does a cold meat sandwich sound good?" Carrie was not one of those people who would let someone go hungry. Brandon nodded, and she instantly went to work fixing him a ham and cheese sandwich and pulled out a soda and a bag of chips. "I'll get you a pillow and blanket from the closet as soon as you're done eating. Then you can go crash on the sofa for the night."

"Thank you so much for doing this for me."

Carrie waved her hand in the air. "It's no problem. We're just glad to have you back."

True to her word, while he was finishing the meal she'd prepared, Carrie brought Brandon a pillow and blanket and laid them out on the sofa. When he was finished, he set his plate in the sink and sat on the sofa.

"I'm heading to bed. I'll see you in a few hours." Mason headed up the stairs with a wave. "Rest well, my friend. I'm glad to have you back. We're going to need you."

Brandon nodded and watched Mason disappear up the stairs.

"He's right. We are going to need you. We'll be down one farmhand come tomorrow. We'll just need to see about hiring some more help once we dispatch with that bastard." Carrie headed for the stairs. "I'm going to be heading to bed now. Do you need anything else?"

"No, I'm fine. Thank you, Mrs. Da... Carrie."

"Okay, good night."

"Good night."

Carrie headed up the stairs and disappeared into her room.

Alone with his thoughts, Brandon spread the blanket and prepared to sleep. But his thoughts kept drifting back to Noah. Was Noah ever going to forgive him for giving the game away? His heart was heavy, and he needed to get some sleep. But sleep was a struggle. How were things going to be between them when Noah came home? Were things going to be awkward? Would Noah never forgive him? Did he just lose the one man in all the world who made his heart flutter?

As these questions swirled around in his head, a restless sleep finally overcame him.

* * *

The sound of pots and pans clanging around awoke Brandon. The light was spilling out from the kitchen door. Brandon sat up and slipped on his shirt before refastening his jeans. The smell of coffee brewing floated into the living room. It seemed Carrie or Mason or someone was up making breakfast. He hoped it wasn't Ian. He was the last person Brandon hoped to run into on the farm, especially after his visit to Caleb's. Ian was going to have a bunch of questions for him that he didn't have answers to yet.

When Brandon entered the kitchen, Mason was already reading the newspaper, and Carrie stood at the stove making breakfast. The sun was barely starting to come up over the horizon, flooding the kitchen with dim golden light.

"Good morning." Brandon came in and took a seat at the table.

Mason grunted a greeting before taking a sip of his coffee and returning to his paper. Brandon knew from experience that Mason wasn't the talkative type first thing in the morning, and he made it a point not to speak to Mason unless Mason spoke to him first.

"There's fresh coffee, and I'm scrambling up some eggs. Why don't you get washed up? Ian should be down soon, and Rick and Mark will be coming in for their breakfast."

Rick entered the kitchen from the side screen door as if on cue. "Good morning, everyone. I... Brandon. Welcome back."

"Thanks."

"Missed working with you, buddy. Where have you been?"

"Away, unfortunately."

Right behind Rick, Mark came strolling in with a cocky grin. When Rick moved to kiss Carrie on the cheek and help himself to a mug of coffee, Mark got a good look at Brandon. His face turned into a scowl. It was as if he wanted to say, "What the hell are you doing here?" but he kept his mouth shut and sat beside Brandon at the table.

God, having that man nearby was making Brandon's skin crawl. But nothing could be done until Mason was ready to make his move. It would probably be best if they didn't say anything and waited. But the waiting was getting dreadful. When was Mason going to say something?

A few moments later, Ian came down. He yawned and sat at the table to Mason's left, which put him right beside Brandon, where Noah generally sat. He did a double take upon seeing Brandon and then stared in astonishment. "Welcome back."

"Thanks."

Breakfast was a quiet affair. No one seemed to want to speak. Once everything was cleaned up, Mason took Mark, Rick, and Brandon, and they headed outside. Mason would give his work-day instructions, and then they would all go their separate ways. He sent Rick to the pasture to work on the fence, as the bull had knocked it down for the hundredth time. He sent Mark to the grain elevator to get feed for the chickens and other farm animals that required it. As usual, he sent Brandon to the barn to work on cleaning up and feed detail.

Brandon headed off to the barn to start working. As soon as he entered the barn, memories began to cross his mind.

Stroking Noah's golden beard and marveling at how soft it was. His lips on Noah's and the hint of chocolate.

Noah resting his head on Brandon's chest underneath the trees. The thought that he may have lost Noah forever was too much.

Brandon's heart hurt so badly. How was he going to make it through without Noah? Was he ever going to come back?

"Alright, where is he?" Mark came walking into the barn, his face twisted into a mask of anger. "Where is my good-for-nothing, son? Did he come back with you? I warned him..."

"He's somewhere you will never find him."

"Good, he can stay there. You stay out of my way, or you'll get the same treatment."

"I wouldn't be making threats if I were you."

"Oh, who's going to stop me? You and whose army?"

Brandon just shook his head and let out a small, annoyed breath. "Your days are numbered. Now, I'm getting back to work."

"Fine." Mark turned on his heel and headed out of the barn.

Brandon pulled off his gloves and rubbed his face with his hands. How could that man be Noah's father? Noah was one of the kindest, most gentle people he knew and didn't deserve to have a father like him.

A few minutes later, Brandon took off his work gloves and wiped his brow, wondering what Noah was doing.

Noah...

Why couldn't he get that man out of his head for five minutes?

It's because you're in love with him and have been for a long time. Yes, he was in love with Noah. There was no way around it at this point. But he had lost him. Would time heal that wound he'd dealt Noah? There was no way of knowing. He'd probably ruined everything.

From outside came a car horn. Brandon put down his rake and headed out of the barn as a car drove up the lane.

Carrie Dale stepped out onto the wraparound porch of the house. She raised her hand to the level of her eyes to block the sun. A sports car came slowly up the drive. Once it stopped, Luke and Caleb climbed out, along with someone else whom Brandon couldn't see at this point.

Brandon made his way up to the car. Hopefully nothing had happened to Noah.

"Oh, my God, this place is beautiful," Luke commented as he looked around.

"It's hard to imagine I nearly destroyed it," Caleb commented as he approached the stairs of the porch.

"I was wondering when you all would get here. I'm about to prepare lunch. I hope you all can stay." Carrie stepped down off the porch to greet her guests.

As Brandon approached, he still couldn't see who the third visitor was because Caleb and Luke were standing in the way. Was it Drake?

As Brandon approached, Luke turned to greet him. "Hey, Brandon. How are you doing today?"

"Doing alright."

"Good. Someone's here to see you."

"Me?"

Luke stepped aside, revealing Noah.

Noah smiled back at Brandon and held up his arms. "Brandon."

Brandon was at a loss for words. "Noah," he barely managed to get out. "I thought you didn't ever wanna see me again. Can you ever forgive me for what I did?"

Noah bit his lip. His face was overcome with emotion, and he nodded. "Yes, I forgive you."

Brandon took Noah into his arms and hugged the man. "I love you, Noah Easton."

"I love you, too, Brandon. And I want you to be my primary. Will you?"

"Yes, I'll be your primary."

"Awwwww," Luke moaned out. "This is awesome."

"So there you are, Noah. You had everyone worried about you."

The sound of Mark's voice made Brandon's blood run cold. He let go of Noah and turned to face the intruder.

Chapter Nineteen

Noah's skin began to crawl as he turned to face his father. "You wretched..." Noah let out a growl and moved to attack Mark, but Brandon grabbed his arm and pulled him back.

"You're all pathetic. You know that. You know he's my son. He's sick. All of you are fucking sick."

"This is coming from a man who beat his wife and child. You're the sick one, Mark." Noah tried hard to wrest free of Brandon's grasp, but Mason put his hand on Noah's shoulder and brought his struggle to a stop.

"Mark Jennings, you're fired. Get your things and get off my property, and if you ever show up again, I will shoot to kill. Do I make myself clear?"

Mark just stood there glaring at Mason with eyes that looked like daggers. "You're going to defend him? Are you as mad as he is?"

"That's rich, coming from the man who nearly beat me in the barn and threatened to burn the house down if I didn't leave. You brought this on yourself; don't tell me you didn't. Did you honestly think I would let you get away with this again?" Noah's rage was almost too much to bear. He pulled his arm free from Brandon's grip, but Brandon quickly wrapped his arms around him.

"No, Noah, it's not worth it." Brandon held on tightly. Damn, when did he get so strong?

"Yes, Noah is my son, but he's sick. He needs to be in the hospital to get him worked out, not on this damned farm being babied. He's a fucking man, not a baby."

"The only sick bastard I see is you. Now, you will gather your things and leave." Mason took a step forward. His chest stuck out. "If you ever come near this farm again or try to contact Noah, you will regret it."

"No worries, Mason. I've just called the police." Carrie came out onto the porch.

"So this is how you deal with your problems, with an ambush." Mark turned his attention back to Noah. "You've done it again, haven't you? You don't know how to leave well enough alone. Why did you have to come back? Why didn't you leave and not come back?"

"Because this is my home. This is my family, and you are nothing but a sick, pathetic drug user. You have no power over me and never will again, you bastard!"

Mark just sniffed the air. "You call me sick, when you're the one being fucked in the ass."

"That's quite enough. I recommend you get moving before the police get here." Carrie stepped up beside Noah and Mason. When Mark didn't move, she said, "Suit yourself. I would love to see them handcuff you and drag your ass back to jail. Anyone for popcorn?"

Mark gritted his teeth and turned to head off to the bunkhouse. "You haven't heard the last of me, Noah. I'm your father. You will never be able to get far enough away from me."

"Let's lay money on that, shall we? You have no power over me, and you will never ever hurt me again." Noah struggled against Brandon's arms, but Brandon held him firm.

"Noah, we are so glad to have you home." Carrie turned to Noah as Brandon released him from his vise grip. "I've missed you around here."

"I've missed you too, Grammy." Noah raced to Carrie and gave her a big hug. Man, he had missed her and her stories and their long talks. She was a delightful woman and more of a mother than his own.

Noah began to think back to Kelly. She had warned him about his father. At least she'd done one good thing in her life. Maybe there was a chance that they could build their relationship again, but it was going to take time. *A lot* of time. Perhaps he could call her in a few days and discuss meeting up. For now, though, he needed to deal with Mark. Mark was still on the property, and until he was gone for good, there was nothing that Noah would be able to do.

A few moments later, Ian came bounding onto the porch, which creaked under his weight. "Noah!" He came running down the stairs and, in one fell swoop, put his arms around Noah's waist and swung him around in the air.

"Hey, big bro, put me down. Put me down." Noah laughed.

"You're back."

"Yes."

"Oh, little bro, I've missed you."

Tears started forming in Noah's eyes as Ian put him back down on the ground. "Big bro, I'm not sure if you know what's been going on, but I..."

"No need to explain. Daddy Mason explained everything to me last night. And before you even ask, yes, I forgive you. You know I will always forgive you for your mistakes. I love you, little bro."

"I love you too, big bro. I also have news." Noah reached out for Brandon's hand and pulled him into the circle. "Brandon and I are going to be primaries."

"Really?" Ian didn't sound even the slightest bit surprised. "Like I didn't see that one coming." He laughed one of his hardy laughs. "I'm very happy for you both."

About that time, Mark came back from the bunkhouse with his things. He glared at all of them before turning and heading for the driveway. Noah guessed he planned to walk back to the city. Before he got ten feet, he stopped as two black and white vehicles with "Remington City Police" came pulling up the drive.

"That stupid bitch called the police!"

Carrie just smiled a sweet smile at Mark. "I did try to warn you. Perhaps next time, you'll believe an old lady."

The officers came up, and an older gentleman approached Mark. "So, Mr. Easton. We meet again. Let's see, breaking a restraining order violates your probation. Attempted battery. We'll be happy to have you with us again."

Mark dropped his things. "Shit."

"Not to mention attempted arson," Noah added feeling more sure of himself, like he was able to finally stand up to his father.

Mark just smiled.

The older policeman who'd spoken raised an eyebrow, clearly interested. "Is that so son? We'll definitely be talking about that soon." Then he turned back to Mark and began to read him his rights. "You have the right to remain silent. Anything you say can and will be used against you in a court of law. You have the right to an attorney. One will be provided for you if you cannot afford an attorney. Do you understand the rights that I just read to you? Do you wish to speak to me with these rights in mind?"

Mark just shook his head as they slapped handcuffs on him.

All Noah could do as he watched this drama was stare. Was it over? Was it all over? Mark was going to jail for breaking his probation and would be under lock and key again. Noah was safe. Safer than ever before. It would be too soon for Noah if Mark ever got out of prison again.

Brandon put his arms around him, and this time, Noah put his head against Brandon's shoulder and watched as the police carted Mark off.

Noah turned to Luke and Caleb when the police cars finally disappeared into the distance. "I promise, it's not always that exciting around here."

Neither Luke nor Caleb said anything. Caleb stepped up to Brandon and Noah. "I have never been so happy to lose houseguests in all my life."

Noah nodded, understanding what that meant. Caleb was a man who guarded his privacy, and he had let Noah and Brandon come barreling into that. Noah pulled out of Brandon's arms and walked over to Caleb. "Thank you so much for putting up with Brandon and me these past couple of weeks. I appreciate everything you've done for me, but this is where I belong."

"I know, sweet boy, but that doesn't mean you can't come to visit me anytime you would like, and besides, Mason and I are primaries. I'm sure you'll see me again soon."

Noah nodded. "One thing this whole experience has taught me is that this is home. Dale Farm is home, and I will never leave home again."

Carrie smiled, and Mason grunted his approval. Ian moved up and hugged Noah again. "And we aren't letting you go again."

"Good." Noah poked Ian's ample belly. "If you ever see me slipping away again, please stop me before I go out of my head."

Brandon coughed at that moment. "I wish you the best of luck with that, Ian."

Ian just laughed.

Noah was home, back on Dale Farm, where he belonged, here with his family.

Chapter Twenty

Once the dust settled, Brandon joined everyone on the porch on the cool summer morning. It was a relief to think that the time he'd spent with Caleb, Luke, and Drake was over, and he was back to work with the man he loved.

Carrie took a seat on the porch swing with Mason sitting beside her. Ian leaned against the wall next to the front door, while Luke took a seat on the steps opposite Brandon. Noah sat between Brandon's legs, with his back against Brandon's chest. It was amazing that he was holding Noah. The man he loved. He almost wanted to pinch himself to ensure it wasn't a dream. Or was it a nightmare? Either way, it was over now, and they were finally home.

"So." Caleb came up on the steps. "I've been teaching Noah about music while he's been away. You should hear the boy sing."

Brandon looked up from his place and saw Caleb holding his guitar.

"Really?" Carrie's eyes were sparkling with delight. "Will you sing for us, Noah?"

"Oh, I don't know."

"Please. I would like to hear you sing."

"Oh, okay." Noah stood up from his place and moved over by Caleb, who started strumming his guitar. After a few bars, Noah began to sing.

"This is my home from home.

My playground of dreams,

Where recess never ends

And the sun throws off its beams
Darkness cannot impede
My childhood dreams.
I have found my neverland
My childhood sanctuary
I have found my neverland
Where I am free and safe
I found my neverland.
When shadows come to call
Life with all its cruelty
I return to my neverland
Where recess never ends.
My place of imagination
Where I began.
I have found my neverland
My childhood sanctuary
I have found my neverland
Where I am free and safe
I found my neverland."

Once Noah's song was complete, everyone applauded.

Carrie folded her hands and put them to her mouth. "That was beautiful." After a moment, she continued. "Who would have imagined we would have our singer in the family."

Mason turned to look at his mother with a smile. "Thank you."

"For?"

"Accepting Noah and Ian as family."

"Of course they're family. Silly boy." She reached out and gave Mason a little pat on the cheek. "They're your boys and, therefore, my grandchildren."

Noah took his seat with Brandon again, and Brandon put his arms around him. "I love you."

"I love you, too."

"So, Luke, what do you think of the farm?" Ian stepped forward and took a seat next to Luke.

"It's beautiful here. So peaceful. I'm so jealous. It's so different from the hustle and bustle of the city."

Mason stood up and moved over to his primary, and the two of them exchanged a quick kiss and embrace. "Thank you for looking after my boy. But next time, let's try to keep the lines of communication open a little better."

"Agreed. The boys need to learn to open their mouths when something isn't right." Caleb's glare was like a searchlight that made Noah cringe, and from the look of it, Ian and Luke as well.

Carrie held up her hand to get Caleb's attention. "Caleb, could you play something for us? We can use some music. This is, after all, a celebration."

Caleb picked up his guitar and started strumming, just as a phone went off.

Luke pulled his phone out of his pocket. "Andy," he said. He held up a hand. "I have to take this. Could you all excuse me?"

"Who's Andy?" Noah asked.

Caleb stopped playing for a brief moment. "That is a very long story. Although why he would be calling Luke is beyond me." He shrugged and returned to his guitar.

The soft melody he played pulled at Brandon's heartstrings, and he hugged Noah close, kissing his neck gently.

Brandon was back home at Dale Farm and happiest with the man he loved. He and Noah would be happy together. Here with their makeshift family. Even Ian didn't seem to inspire the same amount of fear that he'd had felt for him. But that was perfectly okay with Brandon. Ian honestly cared about Noah, and that was all that mattered. He was the teddy bear Noah claimed him to be. It would be nice to get to know him better and find out where this relationship with Noah would go.

"I love you, Noah."

"I love you, too, Brandon."

The two lovers sealed their pact with a kiss.

The end.

About the Author

David Camily is the pen name of LGBT Romantic Suspense author Ryan T. Osborn. He is a native of Central Illinois, who has been interested in writing ever since a very young age. Even though he enjoys romantic suspense the most, he also enjoys romantic comedies and contemporary stories as well.

Read more at https://lordshiningstarr1.wixsite.com/davidcamily.